THE UNSEE

A Thriller

VICTOR METHOS

1

The girl awoke. As her vision cleared, she looked down and saw that she was nude. Her feet dangled at least two feet off the dirty floor. Her head was pounding, and her shoulders screamed. A length of rope encircled her wrists, and her arms were overhead. She was hanging from a meat hook.

Panic began to seep in.

"No," she mumbled, struggling against the rope, "no, please no."

The full horror of what was happening came to her, and she wanted to scream, but *he* was there, somewhere.

Swinging her legs, she gained momentum, and the chains connected to the meat hook rattled. As she fought, she noticed the smell. The smell of rot hit her nostrils like acid and only added to her dread.

She swung her legs harder, grunting with the effort, though she tried to remain as quiet as possible. Twisting, writhing, and fighting, she heard the meat hook rattle as the momentum from her last swing flung her to the bare cement floor.

She rose, her pulse pounding in her ears, and ran to the door. She looked out the small window next to the barn entrance. A farm. She remembered coming to the farm and remembered the drugs… then little else. She looked back. On a metal table against the wall were slabs of meat, buckets of something wet underneath.

She was on a pig farm. She remembered that much—lots and lots of pigs.

Before she turned away, she noticed something in one of the buckets. A horse's tail seemed to be sticking out and running along the floor. But it wasn't a horse's tail. Recognizing it, she slapped her hand to her mouth. Unable to control the sounds coming out of her, she wept.

"Shelly, no!" she cried.

A loud bang in the back echoed through the barn, stopping her heart. Her eyes darted up to the origin of the sound, but there were no lights farther back. Slowly, she backed up until she was touching the entrance. Turning and opening the door just enough for her to slip out, she glanced back and saw movement.

She screamed and ran in the soft dirt and gravel as the sun shone down on her. Because of the drugs, her legs wouldn't move as fast as she knew they could, and she stumbled several times. She heard gravel crackling behind her as someone followed. Screaming, crying, she sprinted with everything she had. She cried out for God to help her, her throat aching from the screams.

A pickup truck sat alongside the home up ahead. She dashed for it, praying that the keys were inside. She got close enough to see her reflection in the window then saw only a blur behind her as pain filled her body and she was thrown to the ground.

"No, please, no!"

A hook had embedded in her shoulder. The shock of looking down and seeing something sticking out of her filled her with a terror she never thought she could feel. Blind, utter horror overtook her as blood began to pour from her wound.

The hook pulled, and she slid along the ground, screaming and kicking. He was dragging her back to the barn.

"No! No! Let me go, let me go! Please. Please!"

The more she fought, the more the hook tore into her flesh, sending waves of pain through her. She felt the gravel tugging at her flesh and the sun warming her body as she lost control of her bladder.

In the shadow of the barn, she tried to tear away, but he grabbed her hair and pulled her inside. She managed to scream once more before the barn door slammed shut, leaving her in darkness again.

2

The parking lot was mostly empty. Detective Ethan Baudin sat on the hood of his Mustang, staring up at a clear blue sky. Cheyenne had some of the clearest skies he'd ever seen, and he'd grown up and lived in Los Angeles his whole life. Though the pollution was going down, as a kid, the black smog hanging above LA had made him think of those cartoons where a dark cloud followed somebody around, and he wondered then if people in LA just weren't meant to be happy.

Having been in Cheyenne for almost eight months, he considered himself a resident. It was beginning to feel like his city, like his people. He'd even bought a black cowboy hat, which he was wearing. The salesman had told him the Cattleman was the most popular style, but he'd gone with the Gus. The hat had a high crown and three indentations, and the salesman had told him the indentations were where cowboys used to grab their hats and take them off when a lady walked into the room. He loved that idea and had purchased it on the spot.

He wore a sleeveless shirt, exposing the tattoos that ran up and down his arms. Some were dragons, others samurai and swords. He had been obsessed with the samurai as a youth, enamored of the idea that there were once men who valued honor and courage above all else—even their lives. He stared down at a red tattoo on his left arm, a samurai lifting a sword as though about to strike.

The car pulled up just then and parked across from him about twenty feet away. The man got out and looked around before approaching Baudin. He was much heavier than he'd looked in the mugshots, and he wore an Arizona Cardinals baseball cap.

"You Charlie?" the man asked.

"I just go by Chuck," Baudin said. "You Eric?"

The man nodded and looked around again. "A hundred pounds. That's what you said, right?"

Baudin nodded as he took out a cigarette and lit it with a silver lighter. "Yeah."

"Come on back."

Baudin hopped off the hood of his car and followed the man. The lot had maybe five cars in it. They were in the lot of an abandoned building that had been for sale since Baudin had moved to Cheyenne. A faded Kmart sign hung over the entrance. Down the block, a Walmart had opened the previous year, and he didn't need to guess what had happened.

As they came upon the car, Baudin saw someone in the passenger seat. A young girl, maybe eight or nine, was wearing a baseball cap, too, and was playing on a phone.

"Daddy, can we go to the game?"

"One sec, baby," the man said, walking over to the trunk. He looked at Baudin. "South High game. My boy's the pitcher."

Baudin looked back to the girl. Her cheeks were red from wind and sun. Her blond hair stuck out from the hat, and she was so engrossed in the phone, she didn't even seem to notice Baudin. Baudin bit his lower lip, his eyes fixed on the girl, who was as innocent as could be. He wondered what excuse her father had given her for stopping in an empty parking lot.

The man opened the trunk, and Baudin quickly walked over and pushed it back down. The two men stared at each other. Slowly, Baudin pulled up his shirt, revealing the mic taped to his belly and chest.

The man's eyes went wide, and his mouth fell open almost comically.

Baudin looked back to the girl and then to him. "Where's the pot?" Baudin asked.

The man didn't move or speak for a moment, then he swallowed and said, "I don't have any."

"Really?" Baudin asked, stepping closer to him and out of earshot of the girl. "Why set this whole thing up if you don't have any?"

"I… I misunderstood. I don't have any."

Baudin nodded. "You sure?"

"Yeah, I'm sure."

Baudin looked back at the kid then took a few steps away from the car. "Well, be on your way then, and quit wastin' my time."

The man hurried into the driver's seat and started the car.

"If I see you again…" Baudin said.

"You won't." The man sped away like a racecar driver. He zipped out of the parking lot, scraping against the pavement, then darted out of sight. In the lot behind Baudin, a van started and pulled forward. The back opened, and two other detectives hopped out.

"What the hell happened?" his partner, Kyle Dixon, asked.

He shrugged. "Sometimes they don't have any pot."

"He said on the phone he had a hundred pounds that he was gonna bring."

Baudin shook his head. "Doesn't work sometimes."

Dixon held his gaze for a second then let it go and went back inside the van to confer with someone else. Baudin sat on the hood of his car and waited until they were done. They were probably reviewing the tape to see if they had enough for a bust. But they would let it go; he was certain of that. So many people were so much easier to catch. They wouldn't waste their time on someone they didn't have a confession on.

Dixon hopped out of the van and came over to Baudin. He put his hands on his hips and spit onto the pavement. He glanced back at the van and made sure no one else was listening. "You and I know if I have a unit pull him over right now, we're gonna find that pot on him. Why'd you let him go?"

"It wasn't for him." He puffed at his cigarette and blew the smoke out of his nose. "It's nine in the morning, Kyle."

"So?"

"So I can smell the hooch on your breath."

Dixon looked away. "So what?"

He rubbed his eyebrow with the back of his thumb, letting the cigarette dangle from his fingers. "Have you talked to Hillary lately?"

Dixon shook his head, staring at the pavement. "No, man. She calls sometimes, but I don't answer."

"You gotta forgive her, man."

"Forgive her?" he said, turning toward him. "What the shit would you know about it? You ever have your wife cheat on you? You ever find out your kid is someone else's? What if someone told you Heather was another man's girl? You forgive your wife?"

He nodded. "Yes, I would. For her to cheat on me, she must've been in enormous pain. I'm not sayin' I'd be together with her again, but I'd forgive her."

He spat again. "Well, you're a better man than me."

"Randy's your son in every way that counts. He doesn't know anything about anything other than he's gonna need a daddy."

Dixon shook his head. "It's too early in the morning for your sanctimonious bullshit. Save it for the afternoon."

After the bust was officially cancelled, they called it a day. In Cheyenne, the detectives didn't have specialties like their counterparts in some of the larger cities. For Baudin, working a homicide one day and doing a drug bust the next was refreshing, kept the job feeling alive. And when he had worked in Robbery-Homicide in Los Angeles, the work weighed him down. It pressed his soul and made him feel like he couldn't breathe. He hadn't felt that in Cheyenne. As soon as a homicide was over, he would move on to a credit card fraud case or a car theft. Nothing ever stayed the same.

He climbed into the driver's seat and waited as Dixon said goodbye to some of the detectives. Dixon looked pale and thin, like he wasn't eating or getting out enough. His clothes were wrinkled and stank permanently of alcohol, his companion since he'd moved out of the home he'd shared with his wife and child. Baudin wanted to be there for him, but sometimes people had to be in pain before they could heal.

Dixon climbed into the car. "You ready?"

"Yeah, man. I gotta make a quick stop, though."

"Where?"

"Just dropping something off to a friend."

3

Baudin pulled up to the Grant View Apartments and parked in front. He stared at the multi-colored brick and stucco. The attempt to make it appear modern just made it look like a mongrel mix of random color.

"Who you got that lives here?" Dixon asked.

"A friend."

"You said that."

"Her name's Candi. She's a workin' girl."

"You're getting a piece of ass now? With me sitting in the car?"

He shook his head. "Nah, man. It's not like that. Just a gift for her. Be right back."

Baudin hopped out of the car and went to his trunk. Inside, underneath the spare tire, was a small baggie of weed from his last bust. He took it and closed the trunk before heading up to the second floor. Candi's apartment was the second one over, a step up from the Motel 6 room she'd been staying in six months ago. He knocked and waited.

Candi opened the door and smiled.

He walked in and laid the weed on the table, along with his hat. "Present for you."

"You shouldn't have." She picked up the bag and opened it, taking in a large whiff. "Never mind, you definitely should have."

Baudin went to her balcony, which overlooked the pool. A man on an inflatable tube was drinking beer, though it wasn't yet ten in the morning. He looked sunburnt. Baudin leaned against the railing.

"People don't see the world the right way," he said.

"How's that?"

"They don't evaluate risk properly. Everything is random, and you got people pounding bells and selling sure things to people that don't know better. It's just perspective. People see the world as much safer than it is."

"How 'bout just asking me how my weekend was?"

He grinned. "How was your weekend?"

"Good. My sister's in town. We're going shopping this afternoon." She sat down at the table and took a pipe out of her purse. She packed it full of weed, lit the marijuana, and inhaled deeply before letting the smoke out through her nose. "How is it you're okay with bringing me weed?"

"It shouldn't be illegal. I'm not in this job to enforce the morality of the corrupt."

"You always talk like that."

He turned to her. "Like what?"

"Like you on some crusade all the time."

He approached her and leaned down to give her a quick kiss on the forehead. "Do you need any money?"

"No."

"You sure?"

"Yes, I'm sure. Business is good. I've got one customer, a regular, feeding me good. Two grand a month for one session a week."

Baudin picked his hat up off the table. "*Customers* and *sessions*, now, huh?"

"I'm movin' up to bein' an upper-class whore, Detective."

Baudin smiled. "Just remember where you came from. I did have one question."

"Shoot." She took another puff off the pipe.

"Mike Sandoval. You heard of him?"

"Hell yes, I heard of him. He's the district attorney."

Baudin nodded, glancing down at the creases in his hat. "I wanna know about him."

"You got access to all sorts of background checks, don't ya?"

"No, not like that. I wanna know about what he's really like. He visits a girl with a white jacket, blue trim. She's not on the corners, but she's definitely a working girl. Escort from one of the agencies. He's been with her two nights this past week. I wanna know who the girl is."

"You think I know all the whores in this town?"

He grinned. "Don't you?"

She blew out a lungful of smoke. "I do. I'll ask around. Why you interested in the DA's extracurricular activities?"

Baudin put the hat on his head. "Because he's part of it."

"Part of what?"

"The blackness that hangs over this city."

She smirked as she looked at him. "And you think you're not?"

"Do you think I am?"

She took his hand and caressed it gently. "No, you're one of the good ones. I just don't want you digging your way into something you might not be able to dig your way out of."

He kissed her hand. "Don't worry about me. But if good people sit by, evil'll win."

"Oh, honey, evil will win anyway."

Baudin stared for a moment then left.

Back in the car, Dixon had his head leaned back on the headrest, his eyes closed. Without opening them, he said, "What was all that about?"

"Just some information I wanted."

"'Bout what?"

"About the dear Mike Sandoval."

Dixon opened his eyes and looked at Baudin. "What are you talkin' about?"

"He's the next one, man."

"Next what?"

"On our list."

Dixon stared at him incredulously. "Ethan, the chief of police was killed because we dug into his life. Everyone's on their best behavior. Whatever you think you know about Mike, you're not gonna find anything."

Baudin started the car. "Maybe. But maybe not."

4

The Mustang stopped in front of Dixon's apartment around six in the evening. He waited a beat before getting out then leaned in through the window. Baudin looked at him.

"I don't think we should do it," Dixon said.

"They started this, man. Not us."

He spit onto the ground before taking out a wad of tobacco tucked between his lip and gums and tossing it into a crack in the pavement.

It was true. Eight months ago, they'd just seen the tip of the iceberg. Sigma Mu, the largest fraternity at the University of Wyoming, had been engaging in rape parties, where they drugged and gang-raped girls. Every member of the frat was forced to participate as a way of guaranteeing no one would go to the police.

But that wasn't what had really bothered Dixon. He'd heard of that kind of thing before. What bothered him was that Sigma Mu had been doing it for well over twenty-five years. Alums of the fraternity included the district attorney, the city manager, several police officers, the SWAT commander, the mayor, a former governor, and several state legislators and senators.

No one would have even known about the goings-on of the frat, except that the chief of police, Robert Crest, got too violent and killed a young woman.

The question was, as Baudin had asked it, how far did the rabbit hole go? How many girls had there been?

Dixon had a lot to say on the subject, but he was tired, and his mouth felt dry. It wouldn't matter what he said anyway. Baudin would do what Baudin thought was right, regardless of whether anyone stood with him.

"You're not gonna let this go, are you?" Dixon asked.

"I dunno. I might get bored of it."

Dixon nodded. "I'll see ya tomorrow."

The Mustang rolled away. Dixon watched it a second then turned to the run-down building his apartment was in. It always smelled like cooking food. Some Africans, Nigerians he thought, lived beneath him, and a little Mexican family lived next door. So his apartment was constantly filled with the scent of frying this and boiling that.

He walked up the stairs to his door and unlocked it. He'd left the air conditioner on. Few things bothered him as much as wasting money when he didn't have to. Money wasn't necessarily tight—he made sixty-two grand a year, and the cost of living in Cheyenne was one of the lowest in the country. But growing up, money had always been tight because of his father's drinking. After his mother ran out on them, the drinking got worse, and every spare dime they had went to that. Dixon had always been the one to turn off the lights or cut open tubes of toothpaste, anything to stretch a dollar just a little bit farther.

Dixon left his shoes by the door and went to the fridge. He was hungry, but all he had were the makings of a sandwich, and he didn't feel like a sandwich. He took a bottle of beer and went out to the balcony. After popping open the bottle, he sat in one of his patio chairs and kicked his feet up on the railing.

The apartment complex was quiet. The only ones who lived there were too young, or too old, to have kids. Dixon liked the quiet. It had been hard to get used to at first, but he found he had trouble remembering what life was like when there had been noise.

He slipped out his phone and went to his photos. He opened a photo of Hillary and stared at it a long time. It was a selfie she'd taken at Disneyland two years ago. Her hair was shorter, but the sparkle in her eyes never faded. One day, he had been in love, and the next, he couldn't talk to her without feeling the urge to vomit.

Her lover, the father of her child, was dead—at Dixon's hands. In a moment of pure rage and panic, he had shot him in the head. He had wanted to call it in, but Baudin wouldn't have it, and Baudin never talked about what happened to the body. Dixon lived with that now. It seemed, in his memory, as though a different person had pulled that trigger. In that moment of pain, he was a different man, and he understood what the term *temporary insanity* really meant.

Dixon breathed out forcefully and turned off his phone. He sat up, guzzled the beer, and set the empty bottle down on the balcony before going to the fridge to get another.

Dixon wasn't sure how long he'd sat on the balcony, but he guessed two hours. Dark blanketed Wyoming. He leaned back in the chair and watched the stars, trying to count them. He'd always done that as a kid, but he'd always lost count after about fifty.

Eight or nine empty beer bottles stood before him. He'd lined them up like soldiers in a firing squad. Reaching out with his leg, he knocked the first one over into the second, and each tinkled then toppled over.

Though exhausted, he knew sleep wouldn't come on its own. Just like every night for the past eight months, he would have to take drugs to force his body to sleep. But before he did that, he wanted to do one thing.

Dixon turned on his phone and dialed his wife's cell.

After three rings, she picked up. "Hello?"

Hearing her voice was like hearing a piece of music he hadn't heard in a long time, a piece of music that had value above being something pleasant to listen to.

"Hey," he said.

A long silence came from the other end then, "Do you have a new phone?"

"Yeah. I lost my other one." That was a lie, but he barely noticed telling it. He'd dropped the other one in the toilet while he was drunk.

"Randy misses you."

Dixon swallowed. He put his hand over his eyes and felt the tears coming, but he fought them back as much as he could. "Yeah... that's, that's too bad."

"Kyle, come over. Come over right now, and let's talk."

"Did you fuck him in our bed?"

"Kyle, don't do this."

"Just answer me," he said forcefully. "Did you fuck him in our bed?"

She hesitated. "Call me when you're not drunk… I love you."

With that, she hung up. He let the phone drop out of his hand.

5

Baudin had never been a day person. The night calmed him. The sunlight didn't comfort him like it did other people. But night cloaked everything, brought down barriers in the mind, and revealed people for what they really were.

He sat on his porch and smoked, leaving the light off so he could see the red tip in the dark. A car pulled up just then, and his daughter, Heather, hopped out. Keri, the mother of Heather's friend Gina, waved to Baudin, and he got the distinct impression that she'd wanted to see him. She was always texting and stopping by to say hello. Though Baudin had the same urges any man did, he had always been better at controlling them than most were. Sex, to him, was a function that occasionally needed to be engaged in, but shouldn't run a man's life. In the end, it clouded thinking, and that was something he wouldn't allow unless it was necessary.

He rose, tossed his cigarette, and sauntered over into the street. He leaned down over the driver's-side window, one arm up on the roof.

"How was she?" he said. "Not too much trouble?"

"Never. She's a dear."

Heather playfully struck Baudin in the stomach then kissed his cheek before running inside the house, waving goodbye to her friend. Baudin looked into the car. He noticed a book about tantric sex lying on the passenger seat. Keri noticed that he noticed, and she was blushing.

"That's for…"

"Research?"

"Yeah. For work."

The two of them looked at each other then smiled.

"That came out so wrong," she said. "I mean, I'm a teacher at the community college. You know that. It's for a class on gender and sexuality."

"Coulda fooled me."

She smiled. "When we going out again?"

"Friday?"

"I'll pick you up. The girls can watch themselves for a few hours."

Baudin stood upright and tapped the roof of the car. Keri waved as she pulled away, and Baudin watched the headlights disappear into the black. He then headed up the porch and went inside.

They had moved after Heather's suicide attempt last year. Baudin didn't believe in the supernatural, but he certainly believed in energy, and certain places just held bad energy. So they'd picked up and bought a rambler in a neighborhood with better schools and more minivans in the driveways. Heather had made several friends, and her grades had improved. She still went to a counselor once a week, but the counselor had assured Baudin that his daughter was doing better.

It didn't help comfort him. No one really knew what another person was thinking or feeling. He still kept a close eye on his daughter.

"You have fun?" he asked, coming to the door of her bedroom as she kicked off her boots.

"Yeah." She paused. "So, are you and Keri boyfriend and girlfriend?"

He smirked. "What makes you say that?"

"I don't know. Gina says she always talks about you. But her grandma said that men like you don't get married."

"I was married to your mom."

"Married again, she meant. Gina said her grandma told her that men like you only have one love in their life, and they never find another."

Baudin leaned his head against the doorframe, staring at his daughter. She looked more and more like her mother every day. The eyes, the nose, the hair, even her thin fingers and middle knuckle that protruded just a little too much… he had to look away.

"Your mother was the love of my life, but that doesn't mean I can't love anybody else. I love you, don't I?"

"Yeah, but it's different." She sighed. "I hope you marry Keri. Then Gina and I would be sisters."

He smiled. "Brush your teeth and get to bed. You have school in the morning."

Baudin went into the kitchen, grabbed a bottle of organic apple juice, then headed to his basement. The wooden stairs creaked when he walked on them, as though they would collapse at any second. He flipped the light switch at the bottom of the stairs and went to the center of the room. A single hanging bulb illuminated the space, and there were no windows. Up on a pinboard were photos of thirty-six men. They had all gone to the University of Wyoming and been members of the Sigma Mu fraternity. At the very top was a photograph of Mike Sandoval, the current district attorney of Laramie County.

Baudin took a step back and sat in a chair. He took out his cigarettes and lit one. He exercised, rarely drank, and never did drugs. He was even a vegan who avoided junk food, but smoking was the one vice he held on to. He'd started in Robbery-Homicide in Los Angeles and hadn't been able to kick it. More than anything else, it kept his hands busy while he thought.

He inhaled and then held the cigarette low, looking through the dim blue smoke at Mike Sandoval's official photo for the district attorney's office. He was smiling, but Baudin could see behind his eyes, could see what drove him. Baudin thought that if he could see what drove a person, their lives would fall into place. Everything around them would make sense. Humans, he believed, weren't random. They were just controlled by forces that seemed random.

"Dad!"

"What, babe?"

"Are you smoking again?"

He put the cigarette out in a paper cup that sat on a table in the middle of the room. "No. Go to bed."

He rose and went to the light switch. Before turning it off, he glanced once more at the photo. He wanted Mike's face to be etched into his memory—the first thing he thought of when he woke up and the last thing he thought of before bed.

He switched off the light and was swallowed by darkness.

6

The sunshine broke through the window and warmed Dixon's face. Grudgingly, he opened his eyes and stared at the ceiling for a long time. Then he threw off the covers, rubbed his face with both hands, and rose.

After using the bathroom and showering, he dressed in jeans, a white shirt, a tie, and a sports coat. He found the ritual of dressing unpleasant, and he wanted to get it over with as quickly as possible. His wife used to help him pick out his clothes every morning.

Dixon took a bottle of scotch from the cupboard and poured himself three fingers in a tumbler. He finished it in two pulls then made toast and smeared peanut butter on it before running out the door.

He drove with the windows up and the radio off. Muffling the rest of the world was better than having to listen to it. It didn't have much to tell him anyhow.

He got to the station just before eight and strolled past the reception desk. The bullpen, what might have been called the "homicide table" in other jurisdictions, was just desks and cubicles shoved together to make room for all the detectives. Dixon sat down at his desk. Baudin normally sat across from him, but he wasn't in yet. He had a new stack of books on his desk with titles like *The Psychopathology of Group Murder* and *Lust Killing Paraphilia: Theory and Investigation*. Whenever there was a slow moment, other detectives were checking on their fantasy football teams, browsing the sports page, watching Netflix, or just talking. Baudin read.

Baudin walked in and collapsed into his chair. Unlike Dixon, he wore a brown leather jacket and jeans. Their captain, Bill Jessop, never said anything about it anymore, not since the chief of police had been killed. Jessop, Dixon suspected, was nervous of what they might find in his background.

Though not a member of Sigma Mu, Jessop had clearly known more about the chief's activities than he'd let on. Just how much he knew might never come to light, but Dixon could never look at him without thinking about it.

"How do you read that shit?" Dixon asked, motioning to the small stack of books with his chin. "That'd depress the hell outta me."

"Gotta know what you're looking at if you're going to understand it. Otherwise, you're just stumbling in the dark." He paused. "You look tired."

"I am tired."

"What time you get to bed?"

Dixon shrugged. "I don't sleep much anymore."

He didn't have too much on his calendar that day. Just a backlog of probable cause statements to write on cases that would be sent to the district attorney's office and screened for prosecution, and then half a dozen reports and supplemental narratives that needed to be drafted. So he stayed at the station all day and wrote, taking only a quick break to run across the street for a sandwich at a café called Fat's.

Baudin did about the same, but he didn't eat. During his lunch hour, he had a smoothie he'd brought from home and read quietly at his desk.

By six o'clock, Dixon's back was screaming, and he sat up and stretched. Baudin yawned as he finished writing something and turned off his computer.

"Wanna get a drink?" Dixon said.

"Sure."

Before becoming a police officer, Dixon had thought it was a myth that cops tended to congregate at certain spots. They allegedly had their favorite bars, their favorite restaurants, and their favorite motels if they needed to sleep one off before a shift. But after only a month at his first job after becoming POST certified, he found it was absolutely true.

My Ex's Joint was a favorite of the detectives division. The dive bar in a dive neighborhood had about the best nachos and Philly cheesesteak Dixon had ever eaten. Most of the space was taken up with pool tables, dartboards, and arcade games. Music was always blaring, and women who either wanted to date cops or had married and divorced one came through every Friday and Saturday night.

A few hollers met Dixon as he led Baudin inside. He ordered two beers on tap then jumped into the fray.

He played pool—he'd found out a few months ago that Baudin was nearly an expert—and drank beer after beer. The pitchers blurred until he realized he was drunk, and on top of that, he felt sick. But he didn't stop drinking.

"No way," Dixon said as he watched Baudin make what looked like an impossible shot.

"Believe it, brother."

"Did you not work in LA? Just play pool?"

"I was undercover with the White Killers for six months, prison gang down there. This is all they did when they got outside, man. Drink, drugs, and pool."

"Six months? Why so long?"

"That's how long it takes to get in with 'em. They were trafficking girls, man. Some of them weren't older than Heather. Just kids being prostituted to the most disgusting, violent men this country has to offer."

Baudin cleared the table as Dixon took another sip of beer, though he knew he shouldn't.

"How's this end for you?" Dixon said.

"What d'ya mean?"

He made a circular motion with his hand. "This whole thing. I seen your basement. You gonna try to bust over thirty people 'cause they belonged to the same frat twenty years ago?"

Baudin shook his head as he sat on the table, the cue between his legs. "Nah, man. We can't get them all. That's impossible. But we can get the key ones. The ones that are still in power, still pulling strings."

"You know what your problem is? It's that you believe in all them conspiracies. You think this is some big fuckin' scam. The chief of police was just crazy. That's all."

Baudin shook his head. "Those girls were raped by dozens of men. And I bet more than one of them has killed."

"Why?"

"Because it's the fantasy, man. People like the ones we're after fantasize about women, then about rape, then about murder. The fantasy becomes everything to them. Then when they kill, it's never as good as the fantasy, and they get depressed. So they get trapped. They're disappointed with reality, but they can't return to fantasy because they've actually acted it out now. They have a crisis of identity, man. They don't know who they are, and they panic. And they try to perfect reality, to make it just like their fantasies. And they'll kill over and over and over, trying to reach that dream of perfection that's unattainable."

Neither of them spoke for a moment.

"You are one upsetting son of a bitch to be around, Ethan."

He shrugged. "Takes one to know one," he said flatly.

7

Walking into the station at eight in the morning, Dixon had a massive hangover and kept his sunglasses on. He took his sports coat off and slung it on the back of his chair. Jessop was in his office, speaking on the phone, and he glanced at Dixon through the glass then turned away.

Baudin was already there, but he didn't have sunglasses. Instead, his eyes were closed as though he were in meditation.

Detective Hector Sanchez came over to their desks and sat down on the edge. "Hangover?" he asked.

"Yeah," Dixon mumbled.

"It's caused by dehydration. You gotta drink more water."

Dixon leaned back in his chair, his eyes turned toward the ceiling. "Or cut my head off."

"That, too." Sanchez took a sip from the Styrofoam cup in his hand. "You boys see that we caught a body last night?"

"No, what was it?"

"Don't know. Some marathon runner saw fingers sticking out of the dirt near Sky Gorge."

"Where?" Baudin asked, opening his eyes.

"Just off I-15. Up a dirt road. Real tucked away. Someone was trying to hide it."

"You got an ID?" Baudin asked.

"No, get this—it's just an arm. We're trying to get some warm bodies together to go up there and search with the dogs. I bet we'll find the rest of him, too."

Dixon swiveled in his chair. "I couldn't give less of a shit, Hector. And no, I'm not goin' up there to search for body parts. He probably got attacked by a mountain lion or something."

He shrugged. "Maybe. Cut looked pretty clean to me." He hopped off the desk. "Suit yourself. I'd rather be out in the sunshine than stuck in here, though."

Dixon opened then closed his eyes again. His muscles felt tight. He used to jog and lift weights, but he hadn't done that since…

The thought of Hillary filled his mind again. Thinking of her was a unique experience—love, disgust, hatred, and lust all at once. He hadn't thought he would feel the lust. The woman had betrayed him as deeply as one person could betray another. But she was beautiful and tender in bed, and Dixon hadn't even touched a woman in eight months.

"Kyle, come with me to get a Coke across the street."

"I'm fine."

Baudin rose. "Come with me."

Dixon sighed. "Why?"

"Just come with."

Dixon grudgingly rose and followed him out of the station. They waited on the sidewalk for the traffic to clear before crossing the street. Baudin lit a cigarette and puffed at it for a moment before turning to Dixon.

"That arm they found," Baudin said.

"What about it?"

He hesitated. "I buried Chris at Sky Gorge."

Dixon stared at him a moment. "But he said he just found an arm."

Baudin shook his head. "I cut him up, man. I buried him all around."

Dixon felt ill and wanted a drink. He didn't want to think about any of that. Not now or ever, but there it was, staring him in the face.

"Should we… tell them?" Dixon said.

"No, man. They got you for murder and me as an accomplice after the fact. Both life sentences, man. You wanna live in a cell? You know what they do to cops in prison, Kyle? They bust out all of your teeth so you can't bite their cocks while they force you to blow them. One after another after another. I'll die first."

Dixon took out his tobacco and stuffed some between his gum and lip. "Is there anything that could lead them back to us?"

He shook his head. "No, I washed the body with hydrogen peroxide. It cleans a body better than even bleach. No physical evidence. But if they ID him, don't you think that's a pretty big fuckin' coincidence that your wife's lover was hacked to pieces and buried in the desert?"

Dixon spit. "This is so fucked up."

"It is what it is. We gotta fix it."

"How?"

"We gotta make sure they don't find the rest of the body."

Dixon went home and changed. He dressed in a long-sleeved shirt and dirty jeans with work boots. He and Baudin had told Sanchez they would help with the search. The news hadn't picked up the story yet, so Jessop wanted an entire body found and an ID made before they did pick it up. They would look like they had a handle on things and that people weren't just dropping body parts in the desert.

Dixon stepped out of his house and saw Baudin in the passenger seat, wearing a sleeveless black shirt and cowboy hat. Dixon got in, turned on the car, and pulled out. He rolled down the windows and turned on a Toby Keith song.

Baudin groaned.

"Not a country fan?"

"I don't like any music where the most popular song is about getting drunk on a plane."

"Says the man in the cowboy hat. The most popular country singers are Johnny Cash and Patsy Cline. You don't think they had somethin' to say? It's just stories. That's all country music is. It tells a story."

Baudin lit a cigarette. "I don't consider Johnny Cash country."

He snorted. "That is just plain ignorant, Ethan. The man was about as country as you can get."

"Shit, man. He's inducted into the Rock and Roll Hall of Fame. That makes him rock." He blew out a puff of smoke. "And he wrote his music—he didn't steal it or have producers write it."

Dixon chuckled. "You think your precious Rolling Stones didn't steal songs or have producers write 'em? Everybody steals from everybody. There's only so many emotions we feel and only so much you can say about 'em."

The drive to Sky Gorge was one of the most beautiful in all of Wyoming. Great expanses of desert met the blue sky at the edge of the earth. When the sun was setting and the sky was the same brownish-gold color as the dirt, telling where one ended and the other began was sometimes difficult.

Dixon took the first dirt road just off an exit near a gas station. It led up past two small hills and into a wide valley. Several police vehicles were already there. Men with T-shirts that said "CPD" in white lettering on the back were huddled in a group, receiving instructions from Sanchez and his partner, Rick. Four German shepherds sat quietly at their feet.

Dixon parked a bit away from them and got out. He and Baudin hiked over without a word then stood at the back of the crowd. Sanchez was going through the search pattern and what they were looking for. The dogs would be spread out, and a few metal detectors would be brought in just in case the vic had on a watch or rings.

Sanchez bellowed, "Any questions? No? Good, let's get this over with. I wanna be home before the Packers game starts."

Dixon and Baudin spread out in a grid search pattern. Slowly, they began to fall back from the others. Within ten minutes, nobody else was within earshot, and within twenty, they were practically alone, far enough away from everyone else that no one could see what they were doing.

"How much you bury up here?" Dixon said.

"Both arms. I cut the fingertips off. I pulled out his teeth, too. They'll send the face to the lab at Quantico for facial recognition. If Chris ever had his photo taken at the DMV, they'll find a match."

Dixon chuckled. "I bet Sanchez doesn't even know what 'FBI' stands for. This is simple stuff, Ethan. They're gonna put out a photo, and if anyone that knew Chris sees that photo, they'll call it in. Including my wife."

Baudin thought in silence. "You okay?"

Dixon looked at him and knew what he was talking about. Dixon had killed an innocent man who had done nothing but love the same woman he had loved. He'd put a bullet in his head and watched the life drain out of him. That kind of thing didn't leave a person, at least a person like him, for a long while.

"Let's just find this damn guy and get outta here."

8

Deputy Sheriff Ben Rivera stopped his car just outside the property. He got out and tucked his shirt back into his pants. In the past year, he'd gained about thirty pounds and didn't really know why. It had happened so gradually that he hadn't even noticed until his clothes didn't fit right anymore and his wife suggested he start cutting out dessert.

He trudged up the hill to the fence. Next to it was a mailbox with the words "The Walks" scrawled across it in black paint. He unlocked the gate, which was just fastened with a bit of wire, then got back into his car and drove up the winding road to the farmhouse.

The Walks' farm sat on about a hundred acres of property just on the outskirts of Cheyenne. Close enough to overlook the city, the place was far enough away that nobody would end up there by chance. The road narrowed, and Ben slowed down before approaching the off-white house surrounded by gravel. A massive barn sat about fifty yards away, and beyond that were livestock pens and a large garden. The Walks liked to eat what they could make or grow on their own farm.

Loud rock music was playing inside the house. Ben stopped and got out, surveying the cars parked haphazardly around the property. He strolled up to the door, watching a few horses farther out, and knocked with the back of his fist. No one answered.

He pounded on the door then just opened it and went inside. At least thirty people were inside, where the smell of marijuana smoke was so strong that it made him want to cough. Some of the women had their tops off or were in their underwear. One woman was completely nude, except for a pair of sunglasses, and strumming a guitar.

"Dennis!" Ben shouted. After making his way through the living room, he looked in the first bedroom, then the bathroom, and walked down a hallway. He opened the door to another bedroom, where Dennis was on the bed, a nude woman bent over in front of him. "Sweet jumpin' catfish, son. Get your damn pants on."

Dennis jumped up and grabbed his mud-caked jeans. He slipped them on and buttoned them as the woman casually rose and began to dress.

She kissed him on the cheek and said, "Same fee."

Dennis nodded and took some cash out of his pocket. He handed it to her, and she brushed past Ben and left the room.

"Boy," Ben said, putting his hands on his hips, "if you had another brain, it would be lonely, wouldn't it? You gonna pay a hooker in front of a cop?"

Dennis looked down to the floor, shifting from one leg to the other. He was slow, always had been, and Ben felt bad that he'd yelled at him. Without the prostitutes, whom Ben had known about for years, Dennis wouldn't have had any female affection in his life.

Ben sighed. "Dennis, you gotta stop with the hookers and find yourself a good woman. Did you go to church like I said?"

For a second, he didn't move. Then he slowly shook his head.

"Where's your mama?"

He pointed downward with his finger.

Ben sighed and looked around the room. "I know you're lonely—we all get lonely—but hookers won't fill that loneliness. Do you understand what I'm saying, son?"

Dennis didn't move, his eyes glued to the floor. He was a large, tall man, with hands that could palm someone's face comfortably. Ben wondered if things had been different, if Dennis could've gone on to play basketball in high school or college. As things were, he doubted Ben would ever leave the farm.

Dennis's most prominent feature was his particularly bad cleft palate. His upper lip was nearly split in half, and the Walks either hadn't been able to afford the surgery when Dennis was younger or hadn't bothered to see a surgeon about it.

Ben left the room and pushed his way through the crowds of prostitutes, drug addicts, and the homeless who knew the Walks wouldn't turn them away. No one seemed to care one bit that Ben had a badge. No one looked nervous or tried to hide the drugs that were in plain view. It was a crowd of people who had lost hope, and nothing made much of a difference to them anymore.

Ben gingerly took the stairs to the basement. He'd once fallen down his own stairs and hurt his back. The basement had been converted into an apartment, though it still had the bare cement floors of a basement. In the corner, pushed in front of a television, was an old woman. Her gray hair was matted, and he could smell the urine on her robe from where he stood.

He ambled over and sat in a chair next to her. Ben sat in silence for a few minutes, watching the game show on television.

"That boy o' yours, Teresa, he is one hell-raiser. Reminds me of his daddy when we was young." He paused. "But he's gotta do something with his life. Idle hands and all. He's addicted to them hookers, and they'll be the death o' him."

The old woman didn't move. She didn't even blink. Her head was tilted slightly to the side, and the quilt on her lap had fallen down. Ben picked it up and put it over her. He couldn't believe the change as he stared into her face. Teresa had been in high school with him, and what a looker she'd been. Ben, pudgy and shy, hadn't even had the guts to ask her to a dance. Now, she looked like little more than a corpse. Teresa was worse than a corpse, because a corpse was obviously no longer animate, but there was still life in her eyes. She just couldn't speak or move, like inanimate, animate flesh.

"Bye, deary."

He walked back up and saw Dennis grab another one of the prostitutes by the wrist and pull her into the bedroom. There was no getting through to him. Hell, Ben thought, if he were in Dennis's situation—born slow and painfully shy because of a deformity, with a papa that drank and abused worse than anything and a mama that was a mute—maybe Ben would have been finding warmth wherever he could get it, too.

He decided he wouldn't be writing any citations that day. He just left the home and shut the door behind him.

9

The search went painfully slowly. Dixon had rings of sweat around his arms, and his collar was soaked. The sun beat down relentlessly, and the air was so dry, he felt as if he were swallowing hot sand whenever he took a breath. The temperature was probably over a hundred degrees.

"Where is it?" Dixon finally asked.

"Another couple minutes this way, under a boulder."

They hiked up a small hill to a massive boulder. It was tilted just enough to fit a person underneath, and Baudin stopped to wipe the sweat off his brow with the back of his arm. He bent down over a small pile of rocks and began tossing them to the side. Dixon watched him for a second then turned away, scanning the great expanse of desert before them.

"This used to be Indian territory," Dixon said. "They found some oil 'bout a hundred years ago, and that was that. Forced them to move and took the land like they was just deer or somethin'. Told 'em to move along. When I was a boy, my daddy told me that the Indians, before they left, cursed the land." He looked back to Baudin, who had moved the rocks aside and was digging with both hands. "You believe that? That a land can be cursed?"

Baudin exhaled and sat back. "It's all cursed, brother. It's cursed because no matter who we are or what we do, it ends in death. The only question we can really ask, the only one that matters, is do we keep going or stop?"

"Stop? You mean suicide?"

"It's the only real question that matters."

Dixon spat and looked back over the desert. "The night after I shot Chris, I thought about it. I can't live in no cell, Ethan. I can't do it."

"You're not gonna have to. What you did was pure emotion from a place of pain. You got nothing to feel sorry over. Anyone in your spot would've done the same. We just gotta fix this and move on." He tossed one of the rocks then sat back in the dirt. "It ain't here."

"What d'ya mean?"

"I mean it ain't here."

"You sure this is the right spot?"

He nodded. "Positive."

"Well, maybe this was the arm they found?"

"No. That was his right arm. His left, I buried here. And it couldn't have been an animal that came and took it. The rocks were put back over it." He paused. "Someone came and got it."

They searched for another six hours. The bottled water they'd brought only lasted half that long. By the end, Dixon's lips felt burnt, and his neck itched. He sunburned easily and regretted not bringing sunblock with him.

By the end, after Sanchez had called it a day, Dixon sat in the car for a while with Baudin and just ran the air conditioner. The air wasn't cold, but it wasn't hot, either, and it felt pleasant on his skin. Then he started the car and pulled away. Neither one of them spoke until they had pulled into the drive-through of a fast-food restaurant and ordered two large waters. As they waited, Baudin stared out at the horizon. Dixon had seen him do that often. He got a certain look in his eyes that told Dixon he was no longer there.

As they rolled out of the drive-through, sucking on their straws, Dixon said, "Were you followed?"

He shook his head. "No, man. No way. At least… I wasn't even thinking of that. There was no one around. I picked some spots on the GPS at random. I didn't think there was any need to look for a tail. But who would do that? No one was there but us."

"Might just be a coincidence. Some sick fuck thought it'd be cool to keep a human arm they found as a trophy or something."

"There are no coincidences."

Dixon kept the air conditioner on the entire drive back. He had drunk his water so quickly that he felt ill and was amazed how something necessary and good could be so bad in excess.

At the station, Dixon collapsed into his chair, feeling nauseated. He would have thrown up if he hadn't thought it would dehydrate him even more. So instead, he went to the break room and found a package of Alka-Seltzer. As he tore it open, he remembered a trick his buddy had told him about in college. He always carried an Alka-Seltzer packet in his wallet. If a girl wanted him to wear a condom, he tore open the Alka-Seltzer. In the dark, it sounded just like a condom wrapper. Dixon had never tried it.

Neither Dixon nor Baudin could really concentrate on work. The sun had a way of draining everything out of a person.

"Assuming it is someone that followed you," Dixon finally said, "what do we do?"

He shrugged. "Wait and see what he wants, I guess."

Dixon exhaled. He opened his email and saw that he'd received fifty-two messages since he'd last checked his email on Monday. He closed his email, leaned his head back, and closed his eyes. His every muscle screamed for sleep that probably wouldn't come.

10

Baudin stayed at the station as long as he could. He had several cases that needed follow-up, but in the end, he just didn't have the energy. The desert had taken everything out of him. He had thought LA was a desert, but now he knew what that actually meant. The desert wasn't about heat—it was about nothingness, an inhospitable environment that tried desperately to extinguish life. He wondered how the Native American populations had turned that place into a home for centuries.

He rose from his desk and told Dixon he would see him tomorrow. As he was about to leave, Jessop bellowed from his office, "Ethan, Kyle, get in here."

He stopped, debating whether to ask if it could just wait until tomorrow. Then he reluctantly turned and headed into Jessop's office. He sat on the couch while Dixon stood by the door with his hands in his pockets.

Jessop sat down and looked from one to the other. Baudin sensed resistance, maybe even a negative energy, mingled with fear. He got the impression that Jessop really didn't know how to feel about the two of them.

"We got a body," Jessop said.

"I know," Dixon said. "We were out with Sanchez all day, looking."

"Not that. A new body. There's some interests here that want this handled quietly, and I told them we would."

A year ago, Jessop would have shouted that order as though it were a commandment. Now he seemed unsure, as if he didn't know how they would respond.

"What interests?" Baudin asked.

"This is rural country. The meat, oil, and leather industries are big here. Employ a lot o' people. They just don't want bad press, that's all. Nothing underhanded."

"What's the body about?"

"Just got the call now. Down at the slaughterhouse. You two head out there. And handle this as quietly as possible. Is that understood?"

"Yes, sir," Dixon said.

They left the office and headed back to Dixon's car.

It was late evening as they drove down to the slaughterhouse. Baudin tried his daughter's cell phone, and she answered right away.

"Hey, Daddy."

"I'm gonna be a little late for dinner, baby. If you want to wait, we can go to that pizza place you like."

"Sure, I'm not really hungry right now anyway."

"Okay. I'll see you in a couple hours. And do your homework."

He slipped the phone back in his pocket and noticed Dixon trying not to look at him. The pain was written clearly on his face. A year ago, he'd had a son and a wife. Now, he had neither. He was alone, and Baudin didn't know how to convince him otherwise.

"She won't wait forever," Baudin said.

"Who?"

"You know who. She'll eventually need a man in her life, and she'll move on."

"Good for her. She should."

He shook his head. "You are about the stubbornest son of a bitch I've ever known."

"How am I supposed to be okay with it, Ethan? You tell me how to be okay with it, and I will."

Baudin watched as the final rays of the sun set and darkness began to swallow the city. "You just let it go. It's not as hard as you think. It's like pulling talons out of your soul. They got you now, but they'll pull out when you let it go."

"I don't think I can do that. When I look at her, I'll always just think of him."

The slaughterhouse, Grade A Meat and Packaging, was off the freeway. Several semitrailers in front blocked the view from the freeway. Baudin knew it was so people couldn't actually see how the pigs were treated.

"You know you can't even film in a slaughterhouse," Baudin said. "It's a felony to film in there. How can you eat something, put it into your body, when the people that make it made it a felony to even see how it's made?"

"'Cause everything that's bad for you happens to be delicious. My grandfather woke up to a beer and fried bacon and sausage every morning, and he lived to be ninety-five. Outlived every vegetarian, vegan, and whatever the fuck I've ever heard of."

"Doesn't mean he felt good doing it." He paused. "You know the Hindus think animals have prana, energy, and if an animal is killed, the energy rots. It turns dark. And when we eat the meat, we ingest that dark energy."

"Yeah, well, maybe they just haven't been over to Pat's Barbeque and had their ribs."

Dixon parked in the visitor lot out back, and they got out of the car. The entrance was a steel door with no windows. The door was locked, but Dixon pressed the call button on the intercom next to it.

"Yeah?" a male voice said.

"Detectives Dixon and Baudin with the CPD."

"Oh, right. Yeah, come on in."

The door clicked open, and Dixon held it for Baudin.

Inside, the smell overpowered his senses. The putridness was something he had never experienced. He began breathing through his mouth, but he could tell from the warm air that he was ingesting something through the air, and whatever it was, he didn't want it.

A few paces in from the door, the darkness took over. He didn't move until his eyes had adjusted. Once he could see, he took in the hanging lightbulbs, the dirty floors, and the rusted metal that made up the entire slaughterhouse.

A man came out of an office, leaning to the side in an awkward gait. The blue cap on his head said Vietnam Veteran.

"I called you guys like two hours ago."

"Sorry," Dixon said, "we just got it. You Henry Peck?"

"No uniforms been out here?" Baudin asked.

"Yeah, there was an officer, but he sat outside for an hour and then said he had to go. Said detectives would be by and not to touch anything."

Baudin shook his head and glanced at Dixon. The murder scene had been left unattended. Baudin had seen things like that frequently over the last year. Murders were so rare in Cheyenne, none of the uniformed officers knew the protocol. He just hoped the scene hadn't been contaminated beyond use.

"Well," Henry said, "follow me."

He led them over a metal bridge that shook as they marched across. Underneath were droves of hogs, all packed in so tightly they could hardly move. They made entirely discomforting sounds, and Baudin thought they sounded like human children.

"Right this way," Henry said.

Beyond the bridge was a wide-open cement floor. Though the floor had been cleaned recently, the black bloodstains that dotted it from wall to wall remained. Baudin kept his eyes up, away from the floor, and observed the equipment instead.

They crossed another metal bridge, and Henry stood at the railing, looking down at a steel vat of meat. Inside the vat was what looked like a metal drill with sharp edges encircling it. The meat, still very bloody, swirled in a counterclockwise pattern.

"What am I lookin' at?" Dixon asked.

Henry pointed to the corner of the vat. "Right there. One of our processors caught it."

Baudin took out his phone and turned on the flashlight app. The bridge splintered off and circled the vat. He strolled around the edge to the corner Henry had pointed at and ran the light over the meat.

Tucked in the corner was the upper torso of a white female. She had been cut in half at the waist and one of her arms was missing. The other arm lay above her head, a tattoo on the wrist. Her face was still mostly intact. Her eyes were milky white and gave her a ghostly appearance.

He turned off the light. "Call forensics out here."

11

The slaughterhouse would've been shut down if the investigation had begun during the day. That would've meant lost work time. Baudin wondered if Jessop had agreed to wait until closing time to send detectives.

The forensic techs mumbled among themselves when they first came out. The theme of the conversation seemed to involve how much of the woman had been ground up with the meat and whether the plant would really do a recall or just let it slide.

Once they began the work, photographs, video, measurements, and analysis of the surrounding meat began. Baudin hung back while Henry gathered a list of employees and anyone who had visited Grade A that day or the night before.

Baudin lit a cigarette and sat on the floor, his back against the wall, while Dixon sat in the office with the man. They were chatting about something, football probably, and Baudin had no interest in listening in. Instead, he closed his eyes in meditation and was gone until the cigarette burned down to a stub and burnt his fingers. He put it out on the floor then tossed it in a trashcan by the office.

"How's it coming?" he asked.

"Thirty-nine employees here yesterday. No visitors. Henry here says they would've noticed a body in the meat right away, so it had to have happened today."

"I don't think it's an employee."

"Why?"

"Because they wouldn't put themselves at risk by bringing it into their work. Unless they're a disorganized-personality killer. But if they're disorganized, they're probably schizophrenic or schizoaffective, something like that, and can't control themselves. They'd be on our radar right away."

"So you're saying someone snuck into the slaughterhouse and shoved that body in there without being noticed and then took off?"

"I'm sayin' I don't know what this is." He paused. "Can I talk to you a second, Kyle?"

Dixon followed him out.

Baudin stopped on the first walkway away from everyone else, and looked at the hogs, which had settled down some. "I don't think we should take this."

"Take what?" Dixon said. "This body? We caught it. There's nothin' we can do."

"We can turn it down. We got enough detectives to hand it off to someone else for a while."

Dixon looked back at the office. "What the hell are you talking about? We caught it—it's ours."

Baudin shook his head. "This type of killer's not gonna be easy to catch, man. It'll take too much time away from the list."

"The list? Are you shittin' me? Your crazy conspiracy theory doesn't qualify as a good reason to turn down a homicide, Ethan."

"The list is all that matters. We have to focus on it. The man that did this"—he motioned to the body in the vat—"isn't anywhere near as dangerous as the men we're after. He can't do as much damage."

Dixon stared at the body as the coroner's people lifted it out of the vat and laid it on a black body bag. "Looks plenty dangerous to me." He exhaled. "Look, just sleep on it, okay? There's not much to do here. You go be with your daughter and just sleep on it."

He shrugged. "All right, but it's not gonna help. The list is all I care about."

"How do you know this isn't part of it?"

Baudin was silent for a moment then looked back at the woman's body. The flesh on her belly where she'd been cut was ragged and torn. All her organs were missing.

Baudin drove down the interstate, thinking about the body in the vat. The woman looked young, maybe twenty. In a small town, maybe people thought they could get away with more or that the police were incompetent and wouldn't catch them. If the murderer was an employee, all the detectives would have to do was interview thirty-nine people and pick the top suspects before grilling them. It was also possible that the killer didn't work there and was clever enough to sneak in and leave the body, hoping the grinder would take care of it. If so, solving the crime would consume Baudin's time and thought, taking his energy away from the list.

In front of the Grant View Apartments, he stepped out of the car. The stairs leading up quivered as he climbed, and he stopped on the top step then looked out over the parking lot. It was quiet there.

He knocked on Candi's door, and she answered, wearing a long T-shirt with no pants. She smiled at him as she left the door open, and he stepped inside. He collapsed onto the lounge chair and checked the clock on his phone. He had to pick up Heather in the next twenty minutes so they could go for a late dinner.

"You wanna drink?" she asked.

"No. Thanks. Did you find anything about my girl?"

"A little. Mike Sandoval has been dating a call girl named Dixie. She works for that escort agency downtown, Glass Toys. He apparently sees her quite a bit."

"You got a last name?"

She shook her head. "Sorry, hon. Rarely last names in this business."

He took out a cigarette. He'd smoked enough today that he had a sour taste in his mouth already, but he needed something to occupy his hands. So instead of lighting it, he just let it dangle from his mouth and pulled it out every few seconds. "That's good enough," he said.

"Now I have a favor to ask you."

"What's that?"

She crossed her legs, and Baudin could see she wasn't wearing underwear. He looked away, and it made her grin. "Some of the girls are frightened."

"Of what?"

"They think we got us a chicken hawk. A john that's been attacking the girls."

"What kind of attacks?"

"Nothin' I've seen. But a couple of the girls went missin' 'bout a week ago. Girls leave all the time, but even among whores, we got friendships. They say goodbye, and we have a dinner or go see a movie or somethin'. These two just left with a john and never came back."

"Did you call the police?"

She chuckled. "Police don't do shit. Other than get free blowjobs. No, I told them I would come talk to you."

Baudin opened a note-taking app on his phone. "Describe the girls and give me their names."

"First one's Shelly. I don't know her last name. Black hair, Asian, real skinny. Has a tattoo of a butterfly on her shoulder. The other one I know better. Hannah Smith, but she goes by Diamond. White girl. A tribal band tattoo that goes around her wrist. Last week, they got into a truck and then was just gone."

"How old are they?"

"Shelly's maybe twenty-five, and Hannah's nineteen."

Baudin froze, his thumb over the keypad on his phone. "What wrist is her tribal band around?"

"I dunno. Right one, I think. Yeah, right one."

He closed the app and opened his text messages. He texted Dixon and said, *You still at the scene?*

Yes.

Send me a picture of the vic's tattoo.

After a few seconds, Baudin got the picture. He showed it to Candi. "That it?"

She nodded. "That's it. How'd you get that?"

Baudin put the phone back in his pocket. "I think I'll take that drink now."

12

The next morning, Baudin swung his feet out of bed, his head still spinning with drowsiness. He forced himself up and to the shower. He brushed his teeth in the shower then pressed his forehead against the tile, staring down at the water swirling over the drain. He didn't know how long he stood there, but when he got out and dressed, he had a couple of voicemails on his phone. One was from Dixon, asking for a callback.

"Hey, you up?" Dixon said by way of greeting.

"Up as can be. What did you need?"

"Got a hit on our body. Ran the prints of the right hand through IAFIS. Her name's—"

"Hannah Smith."

After a long silence, Dixon asked, "How the hell did you know that?"

Baudin went into Heather's room and saw that she had already left for school. He checked the clock on his phone: 10:17 a.m. He remembered waking up at eight in the morning. Had he really wasted two hours already?

"She's a working girl. Candi, the one at the Grant Apartments, asked me to look into her disappearance and she said she had a tribal band around her wrist. I remembered that our girl did, too."

"Shit. So it could be just about anybody in the city and anybody passin' through, huh?"

"The types of predators that target prostitutes want easy targets. Someone that will come back with them willingly because they don't have the charm or the intelligence to get them to the kill spot on their own. It'll be someone that has either mental or physical disabilities. At least a really low IQ."

"So, does this mean you're helping with this body?"

"I don't know. I don't want it to take time away."

"What is it with you and this list? What if you're wrong?"

"I'm not." He paused, catching a glimpse of his reflection in the window over the kitchen sink. "It's here, Kyle. It's spread itself over this city and is eating it alive."

"I don't know what you're talkin' 'bout half the time."

He leaned against the sink. "I just don't know if I can spare the time."

Dixon sighed. "She was a person, too, Ethan. Remember? She's a person. That's what you said about our last vic. She's a person. Well, Hannah's a person, too. You can go chasing men that may or may not be hurting people, or you can stop one that we already know is taking lives. Your call."

Baudin waited a beat before saying, "I'll be down in fifteen minutes."

A silent revulsion filled Baudin, something that he wasn't even sure was really there. As he pulled to a stop in front of the slaughterhouse, he realized his body was reacting to just the thought of smelling the interior of that place again. But he had no choice.

He got out of the car, and instead of going through the door again, he hurried over to a fence on the other side of the building. Poking his head over, he watched a stream of pigs being led from one building to another. They were covered in feces, and several of them had open, festering wounds and bite marks. He'd heard that animals in captivity developed psychosis over time and became cannibals. Some would even kill themselves by bashing their heads into walls.

A couple of employees were herding the animals. One was whipping them, and another was laughing. Baudin watched them until the last pig had entered the other building, then he hopped the fence.

The ground was coated in fecal matter and rotten food. He breathed out of his mouth as he quietly hurried to the door the pigs had disappeared through. Opening it, he was again hit with a smell that made his eyes water. He followed the sound of the men and the pigs, taking each step gingerly and staying far enough back that he might pass for someone just heading in the same direction.

The men walked past several vats like the one Hannah's remains had been found in. Neither of the men looked inside any of them. Most of the vats were off, but a couple were running. The large metal drills spun, pulverizing the meat before it was drained off and sent elsewhere in the plant for further processing and packaging.

The man who had shown them around, Henry, had lied to them. The workers didn't look into the vats. They were like background noise. No one would have noticed a body unless they were examining the vat up close, perhaps while cleaning or prepping for the day.

He headed out of the building then hopped the fence again. Going up to the door, he took a moment to snort out of his nostrils, trying to remove the scent of dead and dying flesh. Then he hit the intercom and was buzzed in.

He went over to where the remains had been found. The vat had been emptied, and the officers and techs had cleared out. Baudin went to the office, where Henry sat staring at a computer screen.

"Excuse me," he said with his best smile.

"Your buddies left a couple hours ago."

"Yeah, I just had a couple of questions of my own, if that's okay."

"Shoot."

Baudin took a seat by the door. Henry had black fingernails, so black that Baudin thought he might've had some disease that was eating away at them. "That vat Hannah was found in, how often do you turn it on?"

"It's on four hours a day in two shifts. It overheats, so you gotta give it a few hours in between."

"How long before the processor spotted the body was it off for?"

"A couple hours. We was gettin' ready to clean it out when he saw it."

"She's not an *it*."

"Excuse me?"

Baudin took out a cigarette and placed it between his lips without lighting it. "She's not an *it*. Her name is Hannah."

"Yeah, I know. I didn't mean nothin'."

"So you don't think she was in there when the machine was on?"

"No way. She'd be ground up like the rest o' the meat."

"Maybe the other half of her was ground up, and you don't want to throw away all that meat. I bet your bosses would be right pissed if you had to do that. Easier to send it out to the public for sandwiches, isn't it?"

The man didn't answer right away. His silence was long enough that Baudin knew he was thinking of what to say. "I don't need this shit. You wanna talk to my boss, go talk to him."

"No, I wanna talk to the man that found her."

13

Baudin stopped in front of the home. It was in a section of Cheyenne he'd driven through but never stopped in. The section had a lot of liquor stores and pawn shops but not much else. He got out of the car and strolled up the lawn. He peeked in a window before knocking. A Hispanic woman answered, a slight fear in her eyes.

"*Habla usted Inglés?*"

"Yes," she said, a heavy accent hanging on the word.

"I need to see your husband."

She opened the door for him, and he stepped through. The home was clean, and paintings of Jesus hung on the walls. The television blared a cartoon in Spanish, and two children sat in front of it, their eyes glued to the screen.

"*Qué están mirando?*"

The children didn't respond. Baudin didn't sit because he wasn't asked to. Instead, he stood by the door and waited, his eyes slowly taking in everything in the home. The man he was about to meet could possibly have killed Hannah. Baudin had seen several cases over the years where the perpetrators of the crimes were the ones to notify the police, hoping to deflect interest in themselves.

Ramon came out in a white T-shirt and jeans. His face was darkly tanned, and his haircut, with certain sections longer than others, had obviously been done at home. Baudin instantly sympathized with him. When he and his wife were newly married and living on the salary of a beat cop, she'd cut his hair at home, too.

"*Yo estoy con la policía. Necesito hablar con usted acerca de lo que viste ayer.*"

He nodded and motioned for the front door.

Baudin stepped out onto the porch and waited as Ramon came out and closed it. He didn't say anything until Ramon folded his arms and asked in accented English, "You here about girl?"

"Yes."

"I don't know nothing. I found her there. That is all I know."

"That's all, huh? *Usted no está mintiendo?*"

Ramon nodded.

Baudin leaned back against the door. "They've already talked to you, haven't they?"

The man averted his eyes and shook his head. "No, no one talk to me."

The fact that the man knew who Baudin was referring to made Baudin think he was on the right path.

"Let me guess," Baudin said, "you're not a citizen. And they told you what to say. If you didn't say it exactly like they wanted, the understanding was that they would call Immigration. *Eso es lo que pasó, no es así?*"

The man looked away. "No. I don't know."

Baudin had seen the same thing a thousand times before. People with illegal immigration status were blackmailed by bosses into doing whatever the boss wanted—whether that was mowing their lawns on the weekends in order to keep their jobs or lying to the police.

"This stays between me and you," Baudin said. "Your name will not be mentioned anywhere other than saying you discovered the body. This conversation will never be known about. I just need to know the truth. She's a person, Ramon. A person. You believe in Jesus, and I know that means something to you. *Usted es Cristiano, y yo sabemos que va a hacer lo correcto.*" The man wouldn't look at him, so Baudin stepped closer, forcing his eyes up. "Did they tell you to say you found her later than you did?"

He hesitated, his eyes on the porch, and nodded.

Baudin lit the cigarette in his mouth. Someone at the plant had forced this man to lie. The rest of the body had been ground up early, probably in an entirely different vat of meat, but they hadn't wanted to waste all that pork.

"What time did you actually see the body?"

He swallowed. "In the morning. I take it to my boss. He come out, and they stop the machines. They take it out and… put it on the side. Then they put it back later in another place."

"They took the body out and put it into a different vat that didn't have much meat?"

"Yes. That meat, the meat we throw away, is the hot dog meat. The… *cómo se dice?* … guts and stomachs, cheap things. Not expensive meat."

Baudin couldn't believe what he was hearing. They'd destroyed a crime scene to save a few bucks. For the first time, he wondered if Cheyenne really was any different than LA.

"Who told you to do that? The man I spoke with last night? Henry?"

Ramon nodded.

Baudin let the cigarette dangle between his fingers. "Thank you for telling me. I promise, no one at your work will know we had this talk."

Ramon nodded and went back inside without meeting Baudin's gaze.

Baudin took out his cell phone before putting out the cigarette. Dixon answered on the second ring.

"Yeah," Dixon said.

"You're not gonna believe this—they moved her body."

"Hannah? Who did?"

"The workers were told to by that fuck Henry. She was apparently ground up in the good stuff, and they didn't want to throw all that meat away. So they pulled out the remains and then put it back later into the vat with all the leftover shit that wasn't worth that much."

"You gotta be shittin' me?"

"We gotta find that meat. Maybe he threw something else in there. Maybe someone else."

Dixon was silent a moment. "Shit. I had a barbeque sandwich for lunch."

"Just meet me down there."

14

Dixon sat on the balcony of his apartment and hung up his phone. He should've told him he'd had too much to drink, but admitting that to anyone, even to Ethan, was too painful. The last thing he wanted right now was to be judged, and even someone as nonjudgmental as Ethan might've had a hard time not doing it.

Dixon rose and went to the bathroom. He washed his mouth out with mouthwash and then splashed on cologne. Then he decided to take a shower because he knew the alcohol had come out of his pores when he sweated.

After a quick shower in lukewarm water, he dressed in a fresh shirt and tie with slacks and a suit coat. Slipping on his sunglasses, he looked at himself in the mirror. He had become exactly what he hadn't wanted to when he was younger: a lonely middle-aged man.

Pushing the thought from his mind, he left the apartment and got into his car. As he pulled out, he saw one of his neighbors heading to her car. The young woman had brunette hair that came down to her shoulders. Her name was Jenny something. She waved. He waved back, and she came over.

"Hey, Kyle, how's it goin'?"

"It's goin'."

"I hate to ask, but you think you can give me a ride somewhere? I was gonna call a cab, but I'd really like to save the cash."

"Yeah, hop in."

She got into the car, and her scent hit Dixon's nostrils. The scent wasn't familiar, not like Hillary's, but it was pleasant.

"So you never told me what you did?"

"Seriously? I usually try to impress all the girls with that right away."

"Oh, this does sound interesting. Let me guess."

He glanced to her. "Take a shot. You'll never guess."

"Well, I wanna say actor, 'cause you've got this, like, chiseled jaw and an adorable smile, but that's not it. You're too down-to-earth to be an actor. It's not anything with your hands 'cause your hands don't have a lot of calluses, so it's something with your mind." She stared at him for a second in silence. "High school teacher."

He chuckled. "Close. I actually wanted to be a high school teacher when I was a kid."

"Why didn't you do it?"

"College wasn't for me. I start reading a book, and I go right out."

"So what'd you end up doing?"

He grinned at her. "I'm a cop."

"No shit. My daddy was a cop."

"No shit?"

"Seriously. He was with the Miami PD for like twenty years."

"So you moved from Miami to Cheyenne? What was that about?"

"It was about getting away from someone that wouldn't go away."

"Oh, one of those."

"Yeah," she said, staring out the window.

A long moment passed before Dixon said, "Well, that's depressing as shit. Can we talk 'bout somethin' else?"

She chuckled. "Sure. What would you like to talk about?"

Dixon dropped Jenny off at the mall, where she worked. He said bye to her, and as she was walking away, she turned back around to say that she hoped she could see him again.

Without thinking, he blurted out, "How 'bout tonight?"

She smiled and agreed.

Driving to the slaughterhouse, Dixon felt something he hadn't felt in almost a year: excited anticipation. Lately, his life seemed like going from one slog to the next. As soon as one chore was completed, another one began. But tonight, he had something to look forward to.

He parked, got out, and saw Baudin sitting on the hood of his car, smoking. Dixon sauntered up to him and sat on the hood. He took the cigarette out of his hand and took a puff before handing it back.

"Those things'll kill ya," Dixon said.

"So will being drunk in the morning."

"I'm not…" He decided it wasn't worth fighting. "So what? It doesn't affect anything."

"If you say so." Baudin hopped off the hood and tossed the cigarette on the ground. "Let's get this over with. I hate this fucking place."

Once they were buzzed in, they found Henry on the floor, directing a few men on one of the machines. When Henry saw them, he rolled his eyes. He rushed over and said, "We've got kind of an emergency here. Can't you guys just call?"

"We need to speak to you," Dixon said.

"It'll have to wait."

He went to turn away, but Baudin grabbed his arm. "Now would actually work best for us."

Henry didn't fight when he saw their faces. Dixon's stare bore into him, letting him know he hadn't made a request. He finally nodded and led them back to the office. Dixon sat down on the couch, wondering if Henry could smell the booze on his breath.

"What do you need?" Henry asked as he remained standing.

Baudin stood in front of him, just a couple feet away. "You lied to us." Henry tried to talk, but Baudin held up his hand, silencing him. "You lied to us, Henry. You impeded a murder investigation. That, by itself, is obstruction of justice. But I don't care about that. See, I don't care about that because I'm thinking to myself, 'Why would someone lie about the death of a girl?' Kyle, can you think of any reason?"

Dixon shrugged. "I guess if they're the ones that killed her, they'd probably lie about it."

"That's what I was thinking, Henry."

Henry's face went slack, and his mouth opened. "What the damn hell are you two talkin' about? I didn't have nothin' to do with that."

"See," Baudin said, holding up a finger, "I think you did. And I think you need to come with us. Now."

Henry recoiled. "No, no, I didn't do nothin'."

"Then why would you lie about it, Henry?"

He swallowed. "It weren't me."

"Someone told you to do it?" Dixon asked.

He nodded. "It was Mr. Walk."

"Who's that?" Baudin said.

"Roger Walk. He's upstairs. He's the owner."

Dixon asked, "What did he tell you to do?"

"I ran up and told him what we found after Ramon told me. He told me to take it out, to not let all the top-shelf stuff be shit on, and then to just dump it in the hot dog meat later."

Baudin turned and began pacing. "That seems pretty callous. He always a callous man like that?"

"Yes."

Baudin turned back to him. "Did he seem surprised when you told him there was a woman's body in one of your machines?"

Henry swallowed again and looked down at the floor. "No, he didn't. But that's just him. He's like that."

Baudin motioned with his head, and Dixon rose.

"We'll go pay him a little visit," Dixon said.

"He ain't here. He's at home."

"We'll find it."

"If you tell him I told you about all this, he'll fire me."

Baudin said, "He won't know. As long as you've told us everything."

"I have."

Baudin stared at him a moment longer then nodded before they left the office.

15

Before heading to Roger Walk's home, Baudin decided they should stop for an early lunch. Dixon reeked of alcohol, and Baudin could tell he hadn't eaten anything by how drunk he was.

They stopped at a diner Baudin had been to several times. The red vinyl seats were new, and everything else was at least fifty years old, including a beat-up jukebox against the wall. When food was ready, the cooks tapped a bell as Baudin imagined they had decades ago. The waitresses wrote everything down on little pads, and even their uniforms looked as if they were from another decade, one that valued modesty more than sexuality.

They sat down at a booth, and Baudin ordered two coffees. For a while, neither of them said anything.

Then Dixon finally broke the silence. "I don't like coffee."

"You need some."

"I'm fine."

"You're not fine. You're about as far from fine as I've seen you."

Dixon watched a couple leaving the diner. They were holding hands, and Baudin could see his partner's eyes focusing on that.

"You ever feel like you're not in the right place?" Dixon asked. "I don't mean in the wrong town or somethin'. Like you're in the wrong time. The wrong century."

Baudin nodded. "I always pictured myself leading the French Revolution."

Dixon chuckled. "I can see that."

"Where do you see yourself?"

"I don't know. Maybe caveman times. When life was just about getting food and getting shelter and nothin' else mattered. You had sex and ate and shit, and that was it. I bet they were happy."

"Maybe, or maybe they were miserable and died early."

Dixon leaned back in his seat when the coffee came. He stared into the cup. "I think I might've always known. I'd look at Randy sometimes and think that he didn't look anything like me. Nothin'. Not an eyebrow, not his nose, eyes… nothin'. But I'd push that thought outta my skull. It was so awful, so fuckin' devastating, I just couldn't believe it. Couldn't believe she would do that."

Baudin took a sip of the coffee. It had a rich aroma and was fresh. "I'm sure she didn't want to hurt you."

"What the fuck is that supposed to mean? How could she possibly think it would do anything but rip my heart out?"

"I don't know. You should ask her."

He shook his head. "I don't… I don't want her to see me like this."

Baudin pushed a menu in front of him. "If she loves you, it won't matter. If she doesn't, then it won't matter, either. You need to eat something."

They ordered grilled cheese sandwiches and ate in silence. After two cups of coffee and a glass of water, Dixon looked much better, more alert. They got back into Baudin's car, and he drove to the address they'd gotten from the Spillman database for Roger Callen Walk.

The home was in an area known as Mellon Road, a section of the city up on a hill that was little more than a cluster of about fifty expensive homes. Baudin guessed they were maybe half-a-million or million-dollar homes, but they would have been worth ten or twenty times that in Los Angeles. Many of the homes had sprawling lawns or entire fields with horses running around. He was surprised the area wasn't gated. Then he remembered that, other than the list, nothing much happened in Cheyenne. But it would. No city was immune from what was coming.

"It's that one," Dixon said.

They parked at the curb. Corinthian columns, white pillars that thrust up about ten feet, ornamented the porch. The door was solid mahogany and about seven or eight feet high. The trimmed plants and bushes on the lawn looked like something from the lawn of a castle, not twenty minutes from downtown Cheyenne.

They walked slowly up the long driveway before coming up to the porch. Baudin didn't see a doorbell, so he pounded on the door with his fist. A woman answered in what appeared to be a gray uniform, but could've been a dress.

"Yes?" she said.

"Is Roger in?" Baudin asked.

"And who are you?"

"The police. Are you his wife?"

"No, I'm the maid. I'll go get him. Wait here, please."

The maid left the door cracked, and Baudin pushed it open a bit and looked inside. The floors were marble, and a painted portrait hung in the living room. A large fireplace took up one wall, and on the opposite wall was an ancient map of the world.

A short man with gray hair and glasses came to the door. He was dressed in a white jumpsuit unlike any jumpsuit Baudin had ever seen. It appeared to be made of silk, and it looked odd with his white tennis shoes.

"I'm Roger Walk."

Baudin flashed his badge. "We just need a minute of your time, Mr. Walk."

"This is about that girl, I take it?"

"Her name is Hannah Smith."

"Right. Well, you might as well come in. I was just sitting down for lunch."

They followed him through the home. Everything was immaculate, polished and scrubbed until it gleamed. Baudin didn't actually think the home was a mansion, but it was decorated like one. As they crossed the massive kitchen to the back deck, Baudin saw a woman in a robe, definitely not another maid, and she didn't smile when she saw him. In fact, she didn't even acknowledge them other than tightening the sash around her waist.

Once outside, Baudin saw the enormity of the backyard. That was really where the wealthy in Cheyenne differed from the wealthy in Los Angeles—land. Almost no one in Los Angeles owned a home with that much land attached. But Roger Walk's yard went on and on for as far as Baudin could see.

"Beautiful property," Baudin said, sitting down in a wicker chair with a fluffy blue cushion.

"It was my father's, and his father's before him. My grandfather came to Wyoming with nothing. He was a wildcat, looking for oil anywhere it was rumored to be. He got lucky here and settled down." Walk took a bite of a croissant that had something white spread across it. "Not to devalue strolls down memory lane, but what exactly do you need, Detective? It is *detective*, right?"

"Yes. What we need is information about Hannah. We found some inconsistencies at the scene, and I thought, 'Who better to straighten them out than the boss himself?'"

"What kind of inconsistencies?"

Dixon said, "Forensics told us that the wounds on her belly were inflicted by your machine. Now, we're not making that public, Mr. Walk. You should know that. That stays between us. I know how important the meat industry is here. But we also gotta find who did this."

Baudin almost grinned. Dixon had played it perfectly. Forensics had said the body was too mangled to be able to tell much, but Walk needed a little nudge in the truth's direction.

"Maybe she was in one of our machines," Walk said. "I couldn't say. I wasn't the one that found her."

Baudin nodded and leaned forward. "See, we can tell when a body's been moved. Lividity. The way the blood settles. After it settles and then the body is moved again, the blood has to resettle, but it doesn't resettle the same way the second time. So we know the body was moved after it had been dumped in your plant. Someone moved it."

"Well, feel free to interview anyone at the plant about that. Anything else?"

Walk had also played his part perfectly. He was an uncooperative cooperative. He had invited them into his home and spoken to them, but not given them a single thing. They would've gotten just as much if he'd slammed the door in their faces, but he seemed to be cooperating.

"Thank you for your time," Baudin said.

They rose and left without looking back. On the way to the car, Dixon said, "Well, that's good that he's not hiding anything."

Baudin got in and stared up at the large house. "This guy's done some dirt. We need everything we can find on him."

16

After pulling up Walk's history, Dixon and Baudin sat at their desks, staring at the paperwork in front of them—an entire life summed up in ten pages. Dixon lifted the stack then dropped it back on the desk just to feel the weight. It didn't feel like anything.

Roger Walk's history, as told by a *Tribune* article, read exactly as Walk had said. His grandfather, Callen Walk, the person he'd gotten his middle name from, had come to Wyoming during the wildcatting days of the early twentieth century. He'd struck oil five years later and sold his rights to the land for a small fortune. The Walks then invested in livestock and switched from oil to meat and dairy.

Roger Walk had three children, two of whom had left Wyoming. One had attended Harvard Business School. The only one who still lived in Wyoming was his youngest son, Dennis. But the file had a note from the Department of Child and Family Services that said Dennis had been taken from Walk and placed with a foster family when he was ten years old. When he turned eighteen, he'd moved in with his biological mother, who was no longer married to Walk.

"No criminal history," Dixon said. "No protective orders, stalking injunctions, not even a call to the cops in his entire life." Dixon leaned back in his seat. "No one's that clean. He's got to have people inside this station helping him."

"He's just rich. The law doesn't apply to rich people like it does to the poor." Baudin rose and paced around their desks. "It would be good cover, wouldn't it? He kills girls then tosses them in with his hogs to be ground up and sold. Gets rid of the bodies."

"This couldn't be the first time at his age. If he's been doing it for a time, why did someone just happen to notice now?"

He shrugged. "Maybe he got sloppy? Ted Bundy said killing was like changing a tire. The first one is easy and clean, everything goes how it should. But by the tenth one, you can't even remember where you left the wrench."

Dixon took a pen and began tapping it against his knee, his gaze on a slip of paper on his desk. "What about the son?"

"What about him?"

"Got taken from Walk's custody. There's probably some abuse there, and he might want to get back at Daddy by dumping a body at his plant. And he would have access to everything."

"So would every employee that has a key to that place." Baudin sat on the edge of the desk. "So the way I see it, either Walk was involved—or someone he cares about is involved, and he's stonewalling us—or he just doesn't want bad press. Somebody else, probably an employee of the plant, did it, in that case."

Dixon sighed. "I think we're gonna have to interview everyone."

"I'll flip you for who calls and gets the interviews set up."

Dixon shook his head. "I got a date tonight. It's all you."

"No shit? A date with who?"

Dixon couldn't help but grin. "A neighbor. Jenny. She's probably half my age, but she's nice."

"She's nice?"

"All right, I wanna fuck the shit outta her. But she's also nice."

Baudin smiled. "Far be it from me to get in the way of new love. I'll set everything. You take off and get showered."

Dixon smelled his underarm. "Not a bad idea."

Once Dixon had left, Baudin sat for a long time at his desk with his eyes closed. Several times throughout the day, he closed his eyes and focused on a single thought. It didn't matter what the thought was, as long as it was simple and he could keep it in his mind. A number worked, but so did a single word, a color, or a note of music. He had once meditated like that for over an hour, and afterward, he didn't know if he had fallen asleep or not.

He opened his eyes and picked up his phone, punching in the number for Grade A. A receptionist picked up, and Baudin asked for Henry, who picked up the line a moment later.

"Henry, this is Ethan Baudin. I'm about to ruin your day."

17

Dixon went home and showered. He hadn't been on a date in so long that he wasn't sure what was proper, especially with someone from a younger generation. In the end, he decided the safest bet was just dinner and a movie. People still ate, and they still watched movies.

He left his apartment and went downstairs. Darkness was quickly enveloping the city. Standing in front of the door, he inhaled the cool evening air and tried to discern the scents he was taking in. Smells were always wafting on the air, whether real or imagined. Sometimes he wondered how much of life was actually in his head and how much really existed.

Shit, he thought. *Now I'm sounding like Ethan.*

He knocked on the door, and Jenny answered after only a few seconds. She hadn't changed her clothes since he'd seen her earlier. She smiled, and it lit up her whole face.

"Lemme grab my shoes," she said.

She picked up some leopard-print shoes and came out of the apartment barefoot. She headed straight to his car, and he was about to ask if she really wasn't going to lock her door then thought better of it. He had to remind himself that not everyone thought like cops did or lived in the same world they did.

"Where we goin'?" she asked.

"I thought we'd grab dinner and a movie."

"Fuck that. Let's go get trashed."

The nearest bar was fifteen minutes away and on the drive over, they talked about what Miami was like. Once there, they sat at the bar, and a crowd slowly began to gather. They met a few other people and began drinking shots. Dixon was older than the crowd they were with, but he didn't mind. The energy of youth was contagious. He felt light and, for the first time in a long time, free.

Two shots turned to five then ten. By the time midnight rolled around, Dixon couldn't remember how much he'd drunk, but several beer bottles were sitting in front of him, and the bartender had already cleared away several shot glasses.

The group they were hanging out with played darts and pool. They danced, though Dixon refused to, and Jenny seemed to be the center of attention. Several of the men danced with her, their hands sliding over her body. But when the other men touched her, Jenny looked at Dixon. Occasionally, she would wink at him, and it made his heart flutter as though he were a teenage girl.

"Dance with me," she finally said a little after midnight.

"I don't dance."

She pressed herself against him, wrapping her arms around his neck. "Dance with me," she whispered in his ear. Slowly, she pulled him out to the floor.

Her body against his, they rocked back and forth, their hands exploring each other before she pressed her lips to his.

Dixon hadn't kissed another woman since he'd met his wife all those years ago. It made his skin tingle, and he wondered if the buzzing in his head was really there. Jenny's lips were soft, far softer than he remembered Hillary's lips being.

Gently, she slid her tongue into his mouth. It was slick and tasted like tequila. He pushed his tongue against hers, and she pulled away, biting onto his lip and pulling with a strength that nearly made him wince.

"Let's get outta here," she said.

Dixon took her hand and led her back to his car.

The moonlight was strong. No clouds were in the sky, and it seemed to go on forever. The stars were almost as bright as the moon was, and Dixon could see them out Jenny's window as they lay in her bed under the thick comforters. A woman's bed... he hadn't been in one for so long that he'd forgotten how much better women smelled than men did. Jenny was asleep next to him, and as quietly as he could, he pressed his face to the pillow and inhaled deeply.

The motion, though slight, woke her. She smiled at him. Her nude flesh appeared pale in the moonlight. Her breasts, supple and round, had pink nipples perfectly in the center. Dixon reached over and ran his fingers around them before putting his mouth to hers. They kissed passionately, then she pulled away.

"Spend the night," she said.

He shook his head. "I can't."

"Why not?"

"I can't sleep. I would keep you up."

"That's okay." She giggled. "Let me help you." She placed her head on his chest and angled her arm so that she could reach the top of his head. Rubbing slowly, she massaged his scalp.

Her face was away from his, so she couldn't see him. The touch felt nice, and the sex had been the best Dixon had ever had. Still, something was missing, and he didn't know what. Everything felt hollow and black.

Biting his lip so he wouldn't make a sound, he wept. The tears streamed down his face as Jenny continued to rub his head until she fell asleep. He removed her hands, then slid out of the bed before putting on his clothes and leaving.

18

Baudin got home late, too late to tuck his daughter in. He turned off the alarm when he got home and grinned because Heather had turned it on. She was taking to heart his lessons about being cautious.

He checked on her. She was asleep in her room, her back turned toward the door. In the moonlight, in that position, with her hair over her shoulders, she looked like her mother. A sharp pain lanced through Baudin like a hot needle stuck into his heart. He shut the door.

After getting a beer from the fridge, he headed downstairs and flipped on the light. The room lit up with the dull glow of the single bulb. He took a swig of beer and sat in a chair before the board.

The beer was cold and stung going down. He closed his eyes and enjoyed the pain for a moment before opening them and rising to his feet. He approached the board and stared at the photo of Sandoval. *You're not getting away from me.*

Hannah's case had done exactly what Baudin had thought it would: distracted him. He had been thinking of Sandoval less and less and about Hannah Smith more. Eventually, Sandoval wouldn't seem as important, though Baudin knew the man was the only thing that mattered.

Baudin hadn't told Dixon, but he had visited their old assistant chief of police, the man under Robert Crest, in prison. When Crest was killed, Internal Affairs and the FBI had opened a full-blown investigation, and the assistant chief, Bill McFarland, was indicted by the US Attorney's Office on forty-two counts of corruption and bribery. After McFarland had been sentenced to thirty years in prison and no longer had anything to lose, Baudin had paid him a visit.

Baudin had to drive to Colorado, to the nearest federal penitentiary. When he actually got into a visiting room and McFarland was brought out, Baudin couldn't believe how much weight he'd gained.

"How the hell you get fat in prison, Bill?" he asked.

The man sat down, breathing heavily, a sheen of sweat on his forehead. "What do you want?"

"I wanna talk. See, you're not part of the frat. I know you don't owe them anything. So I wanted to chat about them."

He snorted. "Fuck them."

He nodded. "They sold you out, didn't they?"

"They needed someone to take the fall, and I wasn't a member. No one believed me when I pointed the finger back."

Baudin nodded. "Help me get back at them. Every conspiracy has a leader—one person that's connected to all the others. Take him out, and the connections disappear. It falls apart. Who is that person? The mayor?"

He chuckled. "Shit. The mayor couldn't find his dick with both hands."

"Who then? I know you know."

McFarland licked his front teeth. "What do I get in return?"

"A clear conscience?"

He laughed. "Shit, man. I took money from one place and put it in another. I don't feel too bad about that. What else?"

Baudin thought a moment. "Because I'm a detective, they give me contact visits with you anytime I want. What do you need?"

He shrugged. "Pot would be nice. But not to smoke—they'll smell that shit. Put it in cookies or something."

"What about booze?"

He shook his head. "We can make booze here in the toilets. Pot and cigarettes have to be brought in."

"I didn't know you were a toker."

"I'm not. But I can trade the pot for other things. Some of the guards will give me extra conjugal visits and shit." He looked down. "Gotta use that shit now before Darlene leaves me and gets remarried."

Baudin leaned back. "You never know. She might stick around."

"For thirty years? No woman would do that." He took in a deep breath and let it out through his nose. "Pot and cigarettes. You bring me that, I'll tell you who you're looking for."

A couple weeks later, Baudin snuck in two packages of cookies made with pot along with two cartons of cigarettes, just enough that McFarland could hide them under his shirt and probably not be noticed. McFarland smiled when he got them.

"You're as corrupt as I am, aren't you?" he said.

"Life isn't about good and evil. It's about choosing the lesser of two evils. You're the lesser of two evils, so I'm helping you." Baudin leaned forward. "Who am I looking for?"

"Mike Sandoval."

"The DA?"

He nodded. "He was one of the founding members of Sigma Mu. I don't know if he started those rape parties, but he was there during the first one, I bet." He smirked. "You know, the chief told me once that he went into that frat normal and came out twisted. He said once you've raped forty girls, you can never have normal sex again. He couldn't get a hard-on unless he was raping them after that. And it just took off from there."

"What's Sandoval's involvement?"

"Even the chief said he was a sick fucker. Said a lot of the girls from the rape parties disappeared. Sandoval used to interview every new hire in the department and the DA's Office. A lotta people owe him their jobs. And sometimes, he'd recruit people right from the prison and put badges on 'em."

Baudin was silent for a moment. "He kills the girls after they rape them?"

McFarland shrugged before glancing around. Then he stuffed the cartons and the cookies under his shirt. "Who the hell knows? That's just what the chief thought. Said he's probably killed somewhere around a hundred girls over the thirty years since he founded the frat."

Baudin thought of that conversation as he stood now in front of a picture of Sandoval and stared into his eyes. That number—one hundred. One hundred lives had been destroyed, and hundreds of children and grandchildren were blinked out of existence because of Mike Sandoval.

Baudin took a step back, looking at the list hanging next to the photo. He'd made a list of everyone in Cheyenne who held or had held a public position and had belonged to Sigma Mu. A name toward the bottom of the list drew his attention. He thought he must've been imagining it, so he took a step closer and stared at the name.

He took the list down, closed his eyes, then opened them again, but the name was still there: Roger Walk.

19

Dixon lay in bed and stared at the ceiling. It was nearly three in the morning, but he knew sleep wasn't coming. So instead, he drank. He'd drunk every beer in his fridge and thought about going to the store to get more, but that sounded like too much of a hassle. He wondered if Jenny had booze, but as he thought about going back over there, his phone rang. It was Baudin.

"Don't you let a man sleep?" Dixon said.

"I just wanted to see if you were up."

"I'm always up." He sighed. "You got any booze? Bring some over. I'm too drunk to drive."

"Yeah, that's not gonna happen." He paused. "Guess who's an alum of Sigma Mu?"

"The President? No, the Queen of England?"

"How about Roger Walk?"

Dixon was silent for a second. "You're kiddin'."

"No. If he's the one doing this, that's why he's gotten away with it for so long. The DA and the chief of police were looking out for him. He's one of them, Kyle."

"Still don't mean he did it."

"You really believe that?" A long silence followed. "That's what I thought."

"So what's the next play? He won't tell us shit."

"I set up twenty interviews for tomorrow at Grade A. We'll start crossing some names off, but I think Walk's good for it. The next play is we start talking to everybody in his life, see what we turn up. And if he's after working girls, we should take his photo around and see if anyone recognizes him."

"How come you always do that?"

"What?"

"Call hookers 'working girls'?"

"Because they are. My mother was a prostitute. The state put me in foster care when I was ten, but I still remember her."

"I didn't know. I'm sorry." He rubbed his forehead. "She still…"

"I don't know if she's alive or dead. Never checked."

"Hmm. Seems like the kinda thing I'd want to know."

"Well, you're not me."

Dixon realized he'd touched a nerve. He swung his legs out of bed and went to the bathroom to urinate. "Sorry. Didn't mean nothin' by it."

"I know. It's just late. Try and get some sleep. We gotta be at Grade A at nine."

Dixon tripped over his garbage can in the bathroom and fell over the toilet. He caught himself against the wall, but not before slamming his head into it and leaving a dent. "Shit."

"You all right?"

He pulled himself up and noticed his body swaying in the mirror. "Better count on me comin' in at ten."

Baudin chuckled. "I'll wait for you."

20

Baudin woke early and made eggs for his daughter. Heather came into the kitchen and sat down at the table. He scooped some eggs with sour cream onto her plate then got her a glass of organic orange juice. He sat across from her and watched her eat.

She noticed and smiled. "What?" she asked.

"I just remember when you were a little girl and would pee the bed. You'd run into my room and slip underneath the covers, trying not to wake me so you wouldn't get into trouble. I always knew you were there, but I let you think you were getting away with it."

She blushed and turned back to her eggs. "Don't be such a dork, Dad."

He reached across the table and lifted her chin so she was looking him in the eyes. "I love you, baby."

"I know."

"Do you?"

"Yes, Dad, I know you love me. I love you, too."

Someone honked, and Heather shoved more eggs in her mouth then got to her feet. Baudin followed her outside and saw Keri in her car, her daughter in the backseat.

Heather shouted, "Bye."

"Bye," he said. Keri waved to him, and he waved back.

Baudin watched them drive away. Heather's childhood had flown by. He could hardly remember when she'd grown up. Next year, she would be getting her driver's license, and they would spend even less time together. He sighed and went back inside to get his firearm and jacket.

Grade A opened at six in the morning, and by the time Baudin got there at nine, several groups of men were already on break. They smoked and ate snacks outside, drinking coffee out of tin cups like he imagined cowboys had a century ago out on the plains. He nodded to them as he parked and got out. They nodded back.

Inside, the room had been set up as he had asked: just a table, three chairs, and nothing else. Interviewing the employees at work was a courtesy he was extending to them. He could've easily demanded that each employee come down to the station and be interviewed individually, but that would mean the men would miss pay. He hoped his attempt to not inconvenience would make them more willing to give him information.

He sat down and pulled out his digital recorder, making sure it was fully charged. He then took a yellow legal pad from his satchel and placed the recorder and the pad on the desk. The clock on his phone said it was just past nine. He closed his eyes and focused on the color blue.

When Dixon finally walked in, he looked disheveled. His shirt wasn't buttoned at the top, his tie had a stain on it, and he had missed a loop with his belt. Even from across the room, Baudin could smell the liquor on his breath.

"Late night?"

"Didn't sleep."

"So you drank instead?"

"Everyone's gotta be doin' something." Dixon pulled one of the chairs to the corner and sat down. He crossed his legs and rubbed the bridge of his nose with his thumb and forefinger. "Who's first?"

Baudin rose and went to the door. He opened it and yelled out, "Elliot Lua?" A moment later, a man slowly marched into the room. He was wearing a denim jacket, and his jeans and work boots were stained from top to bottom with old blood. Baudin motioned for him to sit down, and he did.

Baudin sat across from him. He looked into the man's eyes, and Lua didn't flinch. He didn't avert his gaze or begin to fidget. He wasn't a man who could be intimidated easily.

"You know why we're here?" Baudin asked.

He nodded. "Yes."

"Tell me what you know."

"Nothing. I came later, and they told me a body was found in one of the machines. A girl. That's it."

"How long you worked here?"

"Two years."

"Anything like this ever happen before?" Baudin asked, leaning back in his chair.

"No. Nothing. We had a guy lose a hand, couple guys lose fingers. You gotta be careful, and some of 'em come in drunk. You can't work and drink at the same time."

Baudin resisted the urge to look over at Dixon and see if he'd heard that. "Where were you the night before they discovered the body?"

"With my wife and kids. You can talk to them and ask."

"We will. Do you have a criminal record?"

Lua nodded. "A DUI and some public intox."

"Anything violent?"

"No, never. Not once."

Baudin held his gaze. The man didn't even look nervous. "We'll follow up with your wife and then see if you told us the truth on your history. That's all for now."

Lua rose and left the room.

Dixon said, "That's it?"

"What else can we do? They're not gonna confess. I just want to see how they act."

Dixon exhaled. "Fine. Get the next one so we can get through this. I've got a fuckin' migraine."

21

The interviews took all day, and by the end, Baudin felt as if he'd run a marathon. Every muscle ached, and several times, he'd walked to the bathroom just to get some movement. They ordered lunch in, some sandwiches from a nearby place, and ate quietly in the room. Dixon seemed to grow worse before he got better. He left for the bathroom once, and Baudin could tell he'd gone to vomit, not urinate. When he came back, he collapsed into his chair and said, "How many more?"

"Just Henry."

Baudin called him in. Henry sat down at the table. Baudin could see a trail of breadcrumbs on his shirt and what looked like a cola stain. Henry cleared his throat and hacked phlegm into his mouth before swallowing it.

"You need a drink?" Baudin asked.

"No. Let's just get this over with."

"Where were you the night before the body was discovered?"

"At home. Watchin' TV. *The Tonight Show.*"

"Can anyone verify that?"

"No. I ain't got no wife or nothin'."

Baudin scribbled down on a pad underneath Henry's name that he was unmarried. "Were you ever married?"

"No."

"Any criminal history?"

Henry hesitated. It was only a moment, but that was long enough to pique Baudin's interest.

He looked up, holding his gaze. "Henry, any criminal history?"

"Man can never really move on with you people, can he? They tell me I did my time, and that's that, but that ain't true, is it?"

Even Dixon looked up from his phone and watched the man.

Calmly, Baudin leaned his elbows on the table and stared into Henry's eyes. "What do you have on your record, Henry?"

He ran his tongue along the inside of his lip. "Forcible sodomy conviction from some near fifteen years back."

Baudin hesitated before saying, "What happened?"

"Some crazy bitch I was datin'. She called me over to her house and said she wanted me to fuck her in the ass. That she was ready. I went over there, and I find her in the tub and the lubricant is there. She brought that out. And so I do it, and then we have dinner like nothin' happened. She just says that it was hard for her to sit 'cause it kinda hurt. Next day, detectives are at my house, saying I'm under investigation for rape."

"But you got convicted. How'd that happen?"

"I was lookin' at life in prison. DA said if I pled, I'd do a year and be out. My fuckin' public pretender said I needed to take the deal 'cause she was gonna get up on that stand and cry, and the jury would believe her. Then I wouldn't ever be let out."

"What's the girl's name?"

"Why?"

"Because I'm gonna call her—that's why."

He hesitated and didn't say anything.

Baudin put down his pen. "If I have to go out and find her myself, I'm gonna be really upset, Henry. You would save me at least two hours of searching by just giving me her name. I've shown you a courtesy by allowing you and your men to do the interviews here. You need to show the same courtesy for my time."

Henry looked down to the table. "Her name's Michelle Chesley."

Baudin wrote down the name. "Anything else on your history?"

"Some minor things. Nothing big like that."

"How'd you avoid the sex offender registry?"

"They knocked the charge down so it was just the ten-year registry instead of life. I shoulda fought the damn thing. I didn't do nothin' wrong."

Dixon chimed in, "You visit prostitutes at all, Henry?"

"What? What kinda question is that?"

"So if I took your photo around to the girls down Main Street, they wouldn't recognize you, huh?"

"Hell, no. I don't need to pay for it. I'm in AA, and I meet all my women there."

Dixon glanced at Baudin then said, "We have the forensics people searching the body for DNA. We find even one cell of yours on her, and you're cooked."

"You ain't gonna find shit 'cause I didn't do shit."

Baudin said, "Who was on?"

"What you mean?"

"You said you were watchin' *The Tonight Show*. Who was on the show?"

He looked from one of the detectives to the other. "Don't remember."

"You remember you watched the show but don't remember who was on?"

"No. I'm an old man. Memory ain't what it used to be. Now, are we done? I gotta get back to work."

Baudin hesitated. "Yes, we're finished."

Henry rose and left.

Baudin turned to Dixon. "I think we need to pay a visit to Ms. Michelle Chesley."

22

The day couldn't have ended sooner. Dixon left the plant with a promise to Baudin that he'd follow up with Chesley the next morning and find her current address so they could speak to her.

Grinding pain pounded away in his head. He'd taken enough ibuprofen to put his stomach into knots, and he thought he should get something to eat, though he didn't feel like it. Instead, he drove to a park in the heart of Cheyenne, Lion's Park. He'd gone there sometimes after a shift to decompress before going home. There had to be a demarcation line between work and home. The work was too damaging.

Dixon remembered one case where a mother, addicted to meth, had tied her young son to a chair. The child, no older than a year, kept crying, and so the mother put duct tape over the child's mouth. When the police found him, he was on the verge of death. Deprived of light and food for days, he was so emaciated that Dixon could see his ribs as though he were a skeleton with a thin film over the bones. He couldn't go home after that, pick up Randy, and pretend everything was okay. He needed to get those thoughts out of his head first.

The park was empty. The moon wasn't out yet, but the sky was darkening quickly. He sat on a bench and looked out over the small pond. A cluster of ducks floated lazily near the edge. They showed some interest in him, but when they realized he wasn't going to feed them, they drifted away.

Tears flowed down his cheeks. He hadn't even felt them. He only knew they were there because a few drops dripped onto his hands. He placed his elbows on his knees and leaned forward. Pain had a purpose. It had to. Pain was the body's way of telling the brain the body had an injury. Dixon knew that. But what was psychological pain? His body trying to tell him to deal with something that was bleeding inside?

Leaning back on the bench, he stared up at the sky then decided he couldn't take the loneliness anymore. He got up, rushed back to his car, and drove.

Pulling up to the house, he was filled with an anxiety that numbed him. He stopped in front and put the car in park. Then he chewed gum, hoping to mask the smell of alcohol on his breath. He kept his eyes on the house, on the light in the living room, then got out of the car.

His stomach dropped when he saw the condo across the street. He had killed a man there. Before Chris had died, he'd told Dixon that Hillary and Randy were his family. The rage inside him made him pull the trigger, but looking back on it now, he knew it wasn't rage. It was hurt because he knew what Chris had said was the truth. In a single moment, Dixon had lost the most important things in his life.

Dixon turned away from the condo and trudged up the driveway. Standing in front of the door, he felt as if he couldn't breathe, as if something were crushing him. He swallowed, popped his gum, then knocked.

When Hillary answered, he thought he might pass out. He hadn't seen her in eight months. The only thing that had changed was her hair, which was shorter. The gleam in her eyes, the pearly white teeth, and the supple breasts that thrust out of the tight shirt she was wearing hadn't changed at all.

Dixon felt embarrassed that his first thought upon seeing her was sexual, and he looked away, down at the pavement. "I…"

He didn't actually know what he wanted to say, and now that he was there, nothing came to him.

She reached out and held his hand. "I'm glad you came."

Gently, almost imperceptibly, she pulled him into the home. The house smelled the same. The furniture hadn't changed—nothing had changed. His world had fallen apart, and nothing made sense anymore. But there, the only place he'd ever really considered home, the world couldn't penetrate. Everything had stayed the same.

They sat on the couch, and Hillary waited for him to speak first. She just held his hand and kissed him lightly on the cheek. Dixon had to pull away. He turned his head, and she touched his thigh, letting him know it was okay to look.

"I can't even begin to say I'm sorry," she said. "You're the person I love most in the world, and I hurt you in the worst way."

Dixon opened his mouth to speak, but no words came. Instead, he buried his head in her shoulder and wept.

After a long time, he composed himself and said, "Is he asleep?"

"Yes."

Slowly, he rose then waited for an objection from her, but none came. He crossed the living room and went into the child's room. As he opened the door, the smell that he'd forgotten about struck him—the sweet smell of a child. He waited at the door for a long time before building up the courage to go stand by the crib. He looked down.

Randy looked so much bigger. He wasn't wrapped anymore, but he had a blanket and a pillow. The sight of him made Dixon's knees almost buckle, and he had to grip the crib with both hands as he wept silently.

He felt a hand on his shoulder, then Hillary's arms wrapped around his chest, her head resting on his back. There was nowhere else he wanted to be at that moment, and he closed his eyes and pretended he had never left.

23

The next morning, Dixon woke in his own bed—not the bed at the apartment, but in his home. He opened his eyes slowly and wondered if it all could've been a dream: Chris, the murder, and the drunken haze that he'd lived in. Hillary was asleep next to him. Her hair was short, and he knew it hadn't been a dream. All the pain came rushing back to him in a second, and the weight was back on his chest.

They hadn't made love, but she had held him the entire night. Dixon rose and stared at her for a while before he went into Randy's room. He kissed the boy on the head, then went and sat on the couch in the living room. He didn't know if he was back or if it had been just a night's reprieve in a relationship that had disintegrated beyond the point of resurrecting. And he didn't want to stay and ask Hillary because he was scared he would get an answer he didn't want. So he left.

Sitting in his car, he rested his head back and just breathed, staring at the roof of the car. Before long, the passenger door opened, and Hillary sat down. She was in a robe, a white and blue one he had bought for her while on vacation in Portland. She reached over and gently placed her hand over his.

"I want you to move back in," she said.

"I don't know if I'm ready for that yet."

"I need you. I get so lonely sometimes that I forget I'm alive. Randy's the only thing keeping me sane right now."

He looked at her. "Chris wanted a paternity test. Are you sure Randy's not... I mean..."

"I don't know."

He swallowed and looked away. "I want a paternity test. I need to know."

"Would you love him any less if he wasn't yours?"

Tears welled in his eyes, and he shook his head softly.

"Then what does it matter?" she asked.

"It just does. I want to do it."

She nodded. "Okay. We'll do it. And then after, no matter what the result is, will you move back in?"

Her eyes were wide with either fear or anticipation. She did genuinely miss him. *But if she loved me this much, why did she find comfort in another man's arms?*

"Did you..." *Now isn't the time.* But the time would come. "I'll come over for dinner tonight," he said, "and we'll set a time we can go down and get the test done."

She nodded, kissed him on the cheek, then left the car. Dixon sat for a moment longer, then started the car and pulled away.

After showering and changing, Dixon called the Records Division at the station. They ran a check and got Chesley's current address, occupation—retail clerk at a tanning salon—and her criminal history, which consisted of one conviction for possession of marijuana. He called Baudin and said he would pick him up so they could head down there.

Baudin's new home was better than his old one and in a better neighborhood. When Dixon parked and texted him that he was outside, he looked around at all the houses and wondered what Baudin's neighbors did for a living. It was a solidly middle-class neighborhood, and he was glad Baudin could swing a place like that. Cops in some cities qualified for welfare because they made so little. Luckily, Cheyenne wasn't one of those cities.

Baudin got in wearing a leather jacket with a band around his wrist that had metal spikes on it.

"You goin' to a rock concert or somethin'?" Dixon asked as he pulled away from the curb.

"Wasn't it Seinfeld that said a father stops changing the way he dresses when he has a kid? This is how I dressed when Heather was born, so it's gonna stick."

"So you're tellin' me you're gonna be in a nursing home wearing a leather jacket and a spiked bracelet, zooming around on your wheelchair?"

"I have a feeling those older chicks would dig it."

Dixon grinned. "Facing your own mortality at ninety, and you'd still be thinkin' 'bout pussy, huh?"

"I don't know a better time to think about it." He paused. "No booze this morning?"

Dixon suddenly realized he hadn't had a drink that morning. He hadn't even had the urge. "I guess not."

"What changed?"

He hesitated. "Nothin'."

"If you say so."

They drove around through residential streets until coming to an apartment complex across from a high school. The pavement was cracked, and the metal awning covering the parking stalls was rusted and dirty. The apartments themselves were crammed together so tightly, they looked as though they were leaning on each other. Each building consisted of five floors stacked like Legos.

Dixon parked near the management office then checked the slip of paper he'd written down Chesley's address on. They got out, and Baudin followed him as he headed to Building G, looking for Apartment 1-101.

Dixon knocked then took a step back. The woman who answered had once been beautiful. That shone through, but now, she looked tired. The lines on her face were taut, and she had circles under her eyes. Without makeup, the greasy skin, pockmarks, and acne were visible, and her teeth were beginning to yellow. She was a meth addict—or well on her way to becoming one.

Meth was cheap, and the high lasted a long time. Dixon was old enough to remember when meth had really hit the scene in the nineties. The Department of Child and Family Services had to double their budget because so many children of meth-addicted parents were flooding the system. The state had to come up with the money from somewhere, and several state programs he had believed in, like a program that helped women escape prostitution, had been cut.

"Michelle Chesley?" Dixon asked.

"Yes?" she said shyly.

Dixon showed her his badge. "We're with the police. We'd like to have a word with you, if that's okay."

"I'm heading to work in half an hour."

"We'll just need five minutes."

She nodded and opened the door for them.

They sat down on an old couch covered in stains and cigarette burns. She brought out a chair from the dining table and sat down. She looked nervous, and Dixon guessed she thought they were there about the meth.

"We wanted to talk to you about Henry Peck."

Her face lost all color. She swallowed and crossed her arms as though protecting herself from a blow. "What about him?" she asked quietly.

"We're looking into him for a crime that was committed at his place of employment," Dixon said. "We thought we'd come talk to you about his previous conviction."

Her face turned stern, and her eyes narrowed. "You mean when he raped me?"

Dixon was silent for a moment. "I'm sorry. I don't mean to be insensitive. I just know you have to leave and thought I would get right to it."

She exhaled and leaned back in the seat. Dixon glanced at Baudin and saw that he was watching her unblinkingly, probably analyzing her body language or some other bullshit he thought would reveal something about her.

"What do you want to know?" she asked.

"His version of it was that it was consensual but that you changed your mind after the encounter. I'm guessing there's no truth to that. Am I right in assuming that?"

She shook her head. "That asshole still saying that? Officer, look at me. I may not have model good looks anymore, but do I look like someone that would fuck Henry Peck willingly?"

"Honestly, no. Tell me what happened."

"He was a repairman. Um, a cable repairman. My cable went out, and I wanted to watch my shows, so I called the cable company and told them I needed it fixed. They said they would send someone between two and five. I had a shift at four, so I told them I would leave the door open." Her lip quivered. "I was in the shower when he found me. He stood at the door and just stared. I knew what he was going to do right then." She paused a long time. "He ripped me out of the shower and raped me right there on my bathroom floor. Then he left like nothing happened."

Dixon cleared his throat and looked down at the coffee table. "They cut him a pretty good deal. Do you know why?"

She nodded and rubbed her hands together. "I had some issues, and they thought a jury might…"

Dixon didn't need her to finish that sentence. The prosecution didn't want to risk her criminal history raising the specter during trial that she was being less than truthful. The prosecution had compromised to avoid an acquittal and letting Henry Peck back on the streets with a sense that he could get away with anything.

"I'm sorry," Baudin finally said.

She nodded. "Yeah, me too. You can imagine I haven't had much sleep since his release five years ago. I see him places sometimes. At the coffee shop or a Wendy's or something. He makes sure I see him, and then he's gone before I can call the police."

"When was the last time that happened?" Dixon asked.

"I don't know. A year ago, maybe." She stared off into space for a while. "Makes you wonder, though—how many others there are. If he was a cable man, how many houses could he get into?"

Dixon asked a few follow-up questions then felt it was time to leave. He thanked her for her time and rose. At the door, Baudin whispered in her ear. He took out one of his cards and pressed it in her palm. Then he followed Dixon out.

"What'd you say to her?" Dixon asked.

"I said that if he ever shows himself to her again, I would take care of it."

They got into the car. Dixon sighed and said, "Well, suddenly, Walk doesn't look so good anymore."

"I don't know. Maybe. We need to talk to the prosecutor that handled Henry's prosecution. If there were other girls he did this to, they should've found them. I wanna know why they didn't."

24

The district attorney's office was in the City and County Building downtown. Dixon parked nearby at a meter, and they walked half a block to the building. Inside, a secretary who was popping her gum loudly and sipping on an energy drink greeted them. Baudin asked her for the prosecutor who had handled Chesley's sexual assault, and she searched the computer.

"Oh, wow," she said. "That was one Mike handled on his own."

Baudin's stomach dropped. "Mike Sandoval?"

"Yeah. He wasn't the boss then, though. You'll have to talk to him."

"Is he in?"

"Lemme check."

While the secretary rang up, Baudin looked at Dixon, who shrugged.

"He's in. Go right up."

Most County Attorney offices were split along civil and criminal lines. The civil attorneys handled any issues that arose within county limits and were not explicitly criminal, but Baudin knew they primarily defended lawsuits. Most civil attorneys involved in litigation had an unpleasant disposition. It seemed when money was fought over people were generally unhappy.

The government litigators were different. They didn't work eighty-hour weeks, and it wasn't their money, or even their boss's money, at stake. They gambled with taxpayer money, and that seemed to be enough to take the pressure off. After all, if they lost a lawsuit and had to pay, few people would blame the county. They would blame the person who'd sued them.

On the top floor, attorneys were laughing and joking around in their offices. A few glanced at Baudin and Dixon, but most didn't acknowledge their presence.

"You ever met him before?" Baudin asked.

"Once. In court. He came to watch a homicide trial that was in the news. Seemed nice enough."

Sandoval's corner office was at least three times the size of any other office on the floor. His door was open, and he sat at the desk, flipping through a thick stack of papers. Behind him, an American flag took up a good chunk of the wall, and on the opposite wall were photographs of him shaking hands with people Baudin didn't recognize.

Dixon knocked on the door, and Sandoval looked up. He was an elderly man, maybe sixty-five or pushing seventy. A smile spread on his face, from ear to ear. He rose and thrust out his hand.

"Mike Sandoval, nice to meet you, Detective."

"We've actually met before. The Jackson Dow case, 'bout six years back."

"Oh, right. I do recall that. Domestic violence case, if I remember correctly. You did a fantastic job eliciting a confession from him."

"Thank you, sir."

He held out his hand to Baudin, and they shook. "Ethan Baudin."

"Pleasure," he said, the smile never leaving his face. "Please, have a seat. What can I do for you?"

Baudin said, "We're here on a case of a man named Henry Peck. Do you remember him?"

"Vaguely. Sexual case, I think."

"That's right. He was a cable repairman that sodomized a woman in her apartment when he was there on a job."

"Oh, yes." He leaned back in the seat. "Yes, I do remember that. Nasty case. I believe she had to have reconstructive surgery afterward."

Baudin thought it interesting that the gruesome tidbit was the first thing Sandoval remembered about the case, but he kept his face passive.

"What exactly are you looking at him for now?" Sandoval asked.

"Homicide of two young women."

"Oh. Yes. My screening team mentioned something about this investigation. Found over there at Grade A, correct?"

Dixon said, "That's right. We're trying to keep it as quiet as possible, out of respect for Mr. Walk."

"I'm sure he appreciates that. So why do you think Mr. Peck is involved?"

"Just an unusual history," Baudin said. "That's the reason we're here. The plea deal he took had him off the registry in ten years. Seemed like a sweet deal for someone that did what he did."

Dixon said, "Um, sir, we just think with his history, and that the bodies ended up in one of his machines, we should dig a little deeper into him. What we really wanted to know is if you knew of any other victims."

Baudin kept his eyes on Sandoval as he looked from one detective to another. He picked up a pencil and tapped it against the desktop.

"Yes, Detective, there were others."

Dixon looked at Baudin and then back at Sandoval. "How many others?"

"At least four, that we know of."

Baudin said, "Why wasn't he prosecuted for those?"

"I couldn't get any of them to testify. I think—now I don't have any evidence for this—but I think the son of a bitch threatened them. Ms. Chesley was the only one courageous enough to step forward. But we had some issues with her."

"Like what?"

"Let me look up the case file." Sandoval turned to a computer and searched for a minute. "For one, she'd made allegations against another man for rape about a year before she made the allegations against Peck. Three months after charges were filed and the poor bastard was in custody, she came forward and said that she had made the whole thing up. That she and that man were having an affair, and he called it off, so she wanted to get back at him. You can imagine how that would play to a jury. Also, she had a child, and a DCFS case was pending against her. As part of the case, she was required to do random drug testing. Looks like she tested positive twice—once for methamphetamine and once for cocaine. I was required to hand that over to the defense. It wasn't looking good for a conviction, but I wanted to get something." He turned away from the computer and faced them again. "So, I did the best I could with what I had."

"Do you think you could give us a list of names of the other four women?"

"Certainly. Anything else?"

Baudin was quiet for a second then said, "I noticed you were in Sigma Mu. That must've been hard to see Chief Crest go down like he did."

Sandoval's smile turned into a frown, and he and Baudin stared at each other for a long time. "Yes, I suppose you could say that. I worked with Chief Crest his entire career. For him to turn out like he did… it's just a shame."

"Isn't it, though?" Baudin said.

The two men wouldn't take their eyes off each other, and finally, Dixon had to say, "We'll just get those names from your secretary." He rose.

"Please do," Sandoval said, rising to shake their hands again. "Been a pleasure, boys."

Once they'd gotten the names and were outside, Baudin lit a cigarette and stood on the sidewalk for a second, blowing out the smoke through his nose.

Dixon took a step away. "Do you have to smoke that shit? It's so bad for you."

He shrugged. "I'll quit eventually."

"So?" Dixon said. "Is he the mastermind you think he is?"

"He's definitely hiding something. I don't know about mastermind. I want to get in touch with those girls, though."

25

The first two women on the list had moved out of state. Dixon got their phone numbers from Spillman and left voicemails for both. The other two still lived in Wyoming: one was a schoolteacher, and the other a stay-at-home mom. He printed off their current addresses then met Baudin in front of a grocery store. He got into Dixon's car with armfuls of fruit.

"That your lunch?" Dixon asked.

"Best thing for you."

"So, you're a vegan, but you smoke? You know what kind of shit they put into cigarettes?"

He took a bite of apple. "Couldn't be worse than young girls ground up in pork, could it?"

Dixon had thought about getting a sandwich and fries then eating on the drive over, but he suddenly wasn't hungry.

The woman they were visiting, the schoolteacher, lived about twenty minutes away by freeway, and the school she taught at was just around the block from her home. Dixon turned on the radio, and they listened to Willie Nelson. Dixon had thought it would drive his partner crazy, but Baudin didn't say anything. He just stared out the window, expressionless.

When they arrived at the school, they both got out and turned their gazes on a line of kids walking with one teacher in front and one teacher behind the line.

Dixon guessed his elementary school experience had been a lot different from Baudin's. Having grown up in foster care, Baudin might have seen school as the only reprieve in his life, or he might have gone the opposite direction and rebelled every chance he got.

"Did you like school?" Dixon asked.

"At this age? No. I moved around a lot, sometimes three or four times a year, so I never really had any friends or connections to the teachers. You?"

"Yeah. I actually miss it. No real responsibility, ya know? Just go to school, do enough not to get kicked out, and then have fun the rest of the time. I wish being an adult was that simple."

"Maybe it should be."

They entered the school, and Dixon noticed the low ceilings right away. He wondered if all elementary schools had ceilings that low. When he was a child, the halls of his school had looked massive.

"Excuse me," Dixon said to a woman stepping out of the front office, "we're looking for Mrs. Karen Soccoro."

"And you are?"

"The police. Just a follow-up to something we're looking into. She's not in any trouble or anything."

"Oh, okay. She's in room 112, down the hall and to the left."

Another class marched out of their classroom and stopped in the hall. Dixon couldn't believe how loud they actually were. Several kids were yelling conversations, and a boy with a shirt that wasn't buttoned correctly had his finger so far up his nose it had nearly disappeared.

They turned the corner and found room 112. A woman in a beige skirt and glasses stood at the front of the room, with a map of the United States behind her. She was speaking to a class of what looked like fourth or fifth graders. She saw them and stopped.

"Karen Soccoro?" Dixon asked.

"Yes."

"May we speak with you a moment, please?"

The woman hesitated then told a TA to take over. She stepped into the hall and shut the door behind her. "Yes?"

When Dixon showed her his badge, she had no reaction. "I'm Detective Kyle Dixon. We just wanted to chat with you a second about something. If you could spare five minutes, we'd really appreciate it."

She nodded and opened the door a crack. "I'll be back in a few minutes," she said to the TA. Then she turned to the detectives. "We can talk in the teachers' lounge."

Dixon and Baudin followed her to a room about the size of a classroom. A worn couch sat in the center, and several vending machines were pushed against the wall. Dixon had always wondered if teachers had to pay for their snacks, and it seemed unfair that they did.

Dixon sat down at a circular table and waited until she did the same. Baudin paced around the room, scanning documents and other things lying around.

"I'm sorry to come to your work, Karen," he said. "But we wanted to get this over with as quickly as possible for you. I know it's going to be uncomfortable."

Her eyes went wide. "What's happened?"

"Nothing's happened. We're investigating Henry Peck and were told that you may have been one of his victims."

She folded her arms. "I don't have anything to say about that."

"Is it true you wouldn't cooperate with the DA in Peck's prosecution?"

She shook her head. "I'm afraid I just don't want to talk about it, Detective. It was a long time ago, and I'd like to let sleeping dogs lie."

"I understand that, but we believe Mr. Peck may have murdered two young women. We need to find out as much about him as we can."

She swallowed and looked down at the table. "I wish I could help you… but I can't." She looked from one of them to the other. "Am I free to go now?"

Dixon nodded. "Yes."

Karen rose and headed back into the hall. Dixon listened to her footsteps as she went back to her room. Baudin was touching a handheld massager on the counter. It turned on, startling him. He put it back and waited for a minute to make sure it didn't start again.

"You had nothin' to say?" Dixon asked.

He shook his head. "Not here."

"Well where then?"

"You want people to open up, they have to be somewhere comfortable. She's not comfortable here. I bet she's never told anyone at her work about Henry Peck."

Dixon sighed. "So you wanna hit the last woman on the list?"

"Sure. I've got nothing else to do."

26

The last woman on their list lived three hours away, on the Wyoming-Utah border. Dixon called several times, and no one answered the phone, so they drove to her address. Baudin sat in the passenger seat, and at one point, he fell asleep.

"You drive," Dixon said. "I'm gettin' tired."

They stopped alongside the interstate, and Baudin got into the driver's seat. He drove the rest of the way to a small town that resembled something he might've seen on a '50s sitcom. The lawns were well manicured, and the fences had been painted perfectly. The cars in the driveways gleamed, and Baudin noted appreciatively that no billboards were up anywhere.

"It's amazing how much mind pollution we have to put up with," Baudin said.

"What d'ya mean?"

"Billboards, commercials, emails, texts, mailers… there's no break. To corporations, we're nothing but objects to be manipulated. They don't see us as people."

"Well, then I'm glad they don't run things."

"The entire world is run by corporations and outlaws, man. Everything else is an illusion."

The home was in a cul-de-sac, where they parked and got out. Dixon knocked, and Baudin stepped back to look in the window. While Baudin was scanning the neighbors' homes, a woman in a white-and-blue dress opened the door. Her skin had a faint red tint to it, as if she'd tanned too much before coming to the door.

Dixon put on his widest smile. "Ann Boyer?"

She studied them for a second before saying, "Yes?"

Dixon showed her his badge. "We'd like to talk to you about a matter of some urgency, ma'am."

"What matter?"

"The matter of Henry Peck."

Her face grew stern, and then her eyes narrowed. She took a step back. "I don't want anything to do with that man."

"Ms. Boyer, we're investigating him for a series of new crimes and just trying to get a handle on what happened before. We spoke with the prosecutor at the time, Mike Sandoval, and he said—"

"I can't help you." She slammed the door in his face.

Baudin grinned as Dixon debated whether to leave or kick the door down. He finally decided to knock with the back of his fist, but Ms. Boyer didn't answer.

"We could get a warrant," Dixon said.

"For what? Slamming a door on us?"

"She's hiding something."

"Obviously. But it could be that she's so disgusted that the system let her down, she doesn't want anything to do with us. I'm not forcing a rape victim to talk, are you?"

Dixon put his hands on his hips and looked around the neighborhood. "No, guess not."

Baudin checked his watch. "Let's head back. There's nothing we can do here."

Once back in Cheyenne, Baudin went home and checked in on Heather. She and Gina were studying, and he didn't want to bother them. He asked them a few questions about their day and how school was going then left them alone.

He went down to the basement, lit a cigarette, and sat staring at the photograph of Mike Sandoval. The man had been smooth. Every answer had been perfectly catered for them. Every hair on his head immobile, he had no lint on his suit, and his nails were manicured. Everything had been in its place. Sandoval cared about control more than anything.

When Baudin asked him about the frat, Sandoval hadn't been ready for that, though. No other detective would've asked him about it. He had lost control of the conversation with that question, and for a moment—and just a moment—he hadn't known how to respond. On top of that, talking openly about Chief Crest made him visibly uncomfortable. Baudin had drawn the line. Sandoval was now aware that Baudin knew who he was, and he would probably do whatever it took to destroy Baudin. He'd known it was a calculated risk. The only way to deal with a man like Sandoval was to get him to crawl out of his hole, to come out swinging and make mistakes.

Baudin went upstairs after his cigarette and made a sandwich of veggie ham and mustard. The fake meat tasted bland, but the mustard gave it some flavor. He wolfed it down and followed it with a glass of water before checking in on Heather one more time. The girls were giggling then stopped when he opened the door.

"What's so funny?"

"Nothing, Dad."

"Girl talk, huh?"

"I guess."

"I'm running out for an hour. Do you guys want me to pick anything up on the way back?"

"Couple milkshakes from Shakey's."

"Your wish is my command, daughter."

Baudin headed out the door. Evening was falling, and a chill had accompanied it. The breeze tossed a few leaves along the sidewalks before his house. He watched them for a moment before getting into his car.

He had written Karen Soccoro's home address down in his notepad app, and he put the address into Maps. He set the radio to an ambient station in iTunes and turned up the heat, though it wasn't cold. The car got toasty quickly, but instead of turning down the temperature, he took off his jacket.

Sometimes he missed Los Angeles—the diversity, the ocean, Hollywood, and even the ghettos. But LA was changing. The oceans were becoming more and more polluted, to the point that he didn't think people would be able to safely go into them in the next few decades. Hollywood was built on the movie-making industry, but the movie-making industry was leaving because of the crushing taxes the government of Los Angeles and California imposed. Only the ghettos were constant. Only they were growing.

Baudin watched Karen's townhome for a while. A light on inside—the kitchen, he guessed—went off. Another went on upstairs. He waited a few minutes then got out and knocked.

Karen came to the door in a bathrobe, clutched tightly at the front. She peered over the chain across the opening. "I already told you—"

"He enjoys terror. If he gets away with killing these two girls, he might get around to coming for you next. If you want to die, I won't bother you. But if you want me to stop him, you're gonna have to open this door."

Karen remained silent for a long while. Then she shut the door, slid the chain off, and opened it. Baudin stepped inside.

The townhome was neat and had a grandmotherly feel, with lots of photos on the walls, decorations, plants, and vases. It smelled slightly of incense. She led him through the kitchen and to the living room, which was darker than it should've been because a tree out front blocked the streetlights. Karen sat on the couch, still gripping her robe, and Baudin sat across from her.

"I don't believe for a second that you're the type of woman that would be raped and then not come forward about it."

She stared down at her coffee table, her fingers turning white as she gripped her robe. She glanced up at him then back down. A television was on upstairs, and Baudin wondered if she was married, though she hadn't been wearing a wedding ring the two times he'd seen her.

"I can't help you."

"Why?" Baudin asked. "Who got to you?"

She swallowed. "I can't. I'm sorry."

Baudin leaned forward. "I'm not like other cops, Karen. I don't do things the way they do. I'm here to help, and you can trust me. If you don't want me to tell anyone we talked, no one will ever know."

Karen closed her eyes and mumbled something Baudin thought might've been a prayer.

"He came to my house because some channels weren't working properly. It wasn't this place. I lived in a house then, with my husband. My husband was at work. I was lying in bed, reading, while he fixed the cable. It happened so fast… in an instant. He just ran in and jumped on top of me. He raped me right there, whispering horrible things to me—the things he would do to me if I told anyone." She swallowed again. "When he was done, he went about his work like nothing had happened. He even left a bill on the kitchen counter."

"Was it you that called the police?"

"Yes. I filed a complaint. Detectives came out and talked to me. They said he had other rape charges they were investigating him for and were about to make an arrest."

"So what happened?"

She exhaled. "One night, I was coming into our garage, and I felt this… pressure against me. It slammed me into a wall, and then I felt metal against my neck. And a voice said that I would want to testify against him, but if I did, they would kill me first and then my husband."

"Did you tell the police that?"

She shook her head. "No. I notified the prosecutor that I wouldn't be cooperating."

"Did he ask why?"

"No. He just said it was my choice and that he wouldn't force me."

Baudin wanted to light a cigarette but resisted the urge. "Did the voice sound familiar? Was it Peck?"

"No. I'd never heard it before. It was someone else." She hesitated. "I talked to some of the other girls. This was after. One of them called me to talk about it. The same thing had happened to them. Someone threatened their families."

"But Michelle Chesley came forward."

"She was the only one. They didn't threaten her. I don't know why."

Baudin saw a clearer picture now. Someone had systematically intimidated all of Peck's credible victims, leaving only the one who wasn't an ideal witness to begin with. Peck was an unsophisticated man. Baudin even got the sense that he was downright slow, certainly not clever enough to pull off something like that, particularly since he was probably being held in custody when at least some of the women were threatened. Someone was protecting Peck.

"If you think of anything else," he said, leaving his business card on the coffee table, "you call me directly. Don't speak to anyone else."

"I won't."

"Can I ask one thing, though? That was a long time ago. You still seem plenty frightened to me now."

She walked him to the door. "I got a call two days ago, saying that if I told you anything, they would come after me. I did a star sixty-nine on the number. It turned out to be a payphone at the airport. I think it was the same voice I heard in my garage that night, but I can't be sure."

Baudin nodded, thanked her, and left.

27

Dixon pulled into Hillary's driveway. He was shocked that he thought of it as her driveway—it was his home, the only place in the world he actually considered his home. But it was beginning to slip away and become "Hillary's home." He couldn't allow that to happen. If his own home slipped away from him, he wasn't sure he would have anything left.

He got out of the car and took his time walking to the door. He closed his eyes then opened the door without knocking. She was in the kitchen; he could see her from where he was. After slowly shutting the door behind him, he made his way to the couch. He was about to announce his presence when he saw Randy in a playpen against the wall. The boy's eyes lit up when he saw Dixon, though Dixon figured he didn't know him from Santa Claus. He crossed the living room and picked up his boy. Wrapping his arms around him, he didn't let go until he felt Hillary's hand on his shoulder.

"Sorry," he said.

"I'm glad you came. I was just making dinner."

They sat at the table, with Randy seated in a high chair, which he'd been too small to use when Dixon had lived in the house.

"Did you want to say grace?" Hillary asked.

"You better say it. I'm not feelin' spiritual these days."

She said a prayer over the food, but Dixon kept his eyes open, staring at the boy. Randy could be his son—that was still possible. Maybe Hillary was right, and not knowing was better.

"We can get a paternity test tomorrow morning," she said, seemingly reading his thoughts. "I set it for ten. Can you be there? It's at Cheyenne Regional."

"Yeah…" He paused. "If this is going to work, maybe there's no need to know. Maybe in the end, it doesn't matter?"

She grinned. "He's your son as much as anyone could be, Kyle. But if you're going to always be thinking 'what if,' then it's better to know."

He nodded and picked up his fork. Dixon wasn't hungry, but she had gone to the trouble of making the meal. He took a couple of bites then stirred the food around on his plate.

"You should know, since we're being honest right now, that Chris doesn't live across the street anymore."

Dixon glanced up to her. "No?"

"No. It was really weird actually. He just took off. Someone from his work came by here and asked if I'd seen him."

"No police came by?"

"Why would the police come by?"

He shrugged. "Sometimes they do when people just up and leave."

She watched him for a moment. "I broke it off with him, Kyle. I told him you were my life. You were who I wanted to grow old with. That's why he left. He was, like, obsessed with me. I think he just couldn't handle it. I'm really nervous he'll just show up again one day and try to make claims on Randy."

Dixon nodded, leaning back in his seat, staring at the plate.

"You okay?" she asked.

"Fine. Can we not talk about him, please?"

"I know it must be painful. I'm sorry. I just thought we had to do it at some point. Anyway, I just wanted to let you know he's not around anymore."

Dixon took a linen napkin off the table and brought it to his lap. He rolled the cloth over and over in his fingers, feeling the edges, before laying it across his lap. Randy made a spitting sound then cackled to himself. Dixon smiled, and when he looked at his wife, she was smiling, too.

Dixon spent the night with his wife, though she didn't force anything. As he lay in bed, she curled up next to him and wrapped her arms around him. He felt tears coming again but didn't know why. The urge to drink was back. He slipped out of bed and went to the fridge. She had no booze, so he went to the nearest convenience store and picked up a twelve pack. On Dixon's drive back to Hillary's, Baudin called.

"Don't you ever call during normal hours?"

"There's no such thing as normal anything. Where are you?" Baudin asked.

"Driving."

"Where?"

"Disneyland. What the fuck do you care?"

"Who pissed in your Cheerios?"

He exhaled. "Sorry. I'm spending the night with Hillary and Randy. It's messin' up my head a little. She talked about Chris."

"What about him?"

"She thinks he just picked up and moved away. No cops came out to talk to her about it."

"He probably didn't have any family to file a missing persons report."

"No, not here. He had a mother in New Hampshire or somewhere back there."

"Don't worry. No one's gonna find out anything."

"Oh, really? Someone dug him up from the desert, and you think no one's gonna know anything, huh? This type of shit has a way of coming back to haunt you, Ethan. If not physically…"

"Psychologically? You feeling guilty about what you did? Is that what all this bullshit is about?"

Dixon was silent for a moment as he pulled onto his street. "I killed him like he was nothin'. I should be in prison."

"You wouldn't be in prison alone—I'd be there, too. And your wife and my daughter would be left alone in this darkness. So let's cut all this shit about feelin' bad. What happened, happened. You can't change it, so feeling anxious about it is useless."

"Easier said than done, brother. I better go. I'm pullin' into my house."

Dixon got out of the car with the booze and headed inside. He glanced back once at Chris's condo, and the sight filled him with a dull gray dread. He turned around and decided that if his relationship with Hillary was going to work, they would have to move.

28

Baudin woke early, while it was still dark. He showered and got an apple from the kitchen before giving Heather a kiss on his way out the door. The early-morning sky was different from the night sky, though both were black and speckled with stars. Some hint of daylight permeated the blackness, making it seem somehow less majestic, less enigmatic. The night held secrets the day couldn't touch. Baudin had read that in a poem somewhere and could never remember where.

The morning shift at Grade A started in an hour. Baudin drove quickly on the freeway, which he'd thought would be empty, but he shared the road with more cars than he'd seen at most other times of the day. Blue-collar workers were usually forced to wake before everyone else. He doubted many stockbrokers or CEOs were on the freeway that early.

At Grade A, he parked out front. He didn't expect Peck to confess to him, but maybe Baudin could unnerve him enough to force him to make a mistake. He might get some sort of information to land a search warrant for Peck's home. Baudin had no doubt a killer like Peck had taken a souvenir. Sex killers always needed to relive their killings, to masturbate while reenacting them. He wouldn't have been surprised if Peck had videos of the killings stashed somewhere in his home.

Baudin leaned his head back and listened to soothing opera, something by Puccini, and let his thoughts drift on the music. They floated around his daughter and his fears for her. One day, she would have to be off into the world by herself. He was nervous that he hadn't prepared her. She was his only child, the single thing he had left that reminded him of his wife. He had shielded Heather from the world as best he could, and in doing so, he might've taken away situations that could've made her stronger.

When he opened his eyes, a half hour had passed. Baudin watched workers filing into the plant for a good ten minutes before he saw Peck. The man wore jeans, a beige shirt with work boots, and a beige cap with the illustration of a fish caught on a hook. Baudin stepped out of the car. As Baudin approached the line of workers, Peck saw him.

Something had changed. Peck's eyes went wide, and he froze.

Baudin stopped, too, suddenly feeling the need to reach for his sidearm, but he resisted. As calmly as he could, he said, "Henry, I just need to talk."

He didn't know if it had been his demeanor, the way he walked or moved, but something had told Peck that Baudin knew. And Peck ran. He pushed aside the other workers and dashed into the plant.

Baudin shouted, "Hey!" Then he had no choice but to run in. He shoved his way through a small crowd milling around at the door. Inside the plant, most of the lights were off, and the darkness was impenetrable except for a few lights on over the line of workers waiting to clock in. Baudin ran up to the edge of the light as far as he could and scanned from one end of the plant to the other. He heard footfalls in the darkness and dashed toward the sound.

"Henry, I just want to talk," he shouted.

The footfalls grew faster. Baudin sped up, too. Then he smashed into a railing he couldn't see. He nearly tumbled over and only stopped himself by gripping the railing at the last moment. His momentum carried him over, and he held the railing with both hands, holding himself suspended over a vat.

The footfalls barreled toward him. Baudin hauled himself up just as something metal—probably a shovel—slammed into his cheek and sent him sprawling backward. He fell into an empty vat with a massive gong sound and rolled as he slid down the side. His vision swirled, and he saw Peck's silhouette toss the shovel and run.

It took him a moment to regain his balance and pull himself up. The sides of the vat had been cleaned and oiled, and he had to use hands, knees, and feet to get to the edge and reach the railing again. Heaving himself over the railing, he thrust out one foot and landed hard. Dizzy, he stood up straight.

Baudin hurried through the darkness until he remembered the flashlight app on his phone. He took it out and lit an area about six feet around him. He could hear the workers across the plant talking and see the light track they were walking down, but he knew they couldn't see him. He thought about calling it in, but Peck made it personal.

Baudin ran to the wall and followed it down. At the thick steel door to the left, he closed his eyes and listened, trying to tell if anyone was still near him. If he didn't want to keep exploring in the dark, the door was his only choice.

He opened the door. The area beyond seemed to be a processing room. Multiple machines took up the space, and he wasn't quite sure what they were used for. Nobody was inside, and once the door shut, he couldn't hear the voices of the workers anymore.

"Henry, I don't know why you ran, but if you stop right now and talk to me, we'll pretend this little incident didn't happen. I just want to talk."

Baudin slipped out his sidearm and held it low. He didn't feel any blood trickling down his face, but the left side of his head burned, and he knew it was swelling up.

"Henry, come out. We can talk right here if you want. Away from everyone else."

He listened for a solid half a minute but didn't hear anything. Slowly, Baudin eased around the machines. He could see hooks and grips attached to large metal plates that looked as though they could spin. He suddenly recognized the machines' purpose—holding livestock upside down while their throats were slit.

The lights were little more than bulbs surrounded by red cones to spread the light farther in the room. Little electric crackles emanated from them. He lifted his sidearm about chest high. "Henry, just talk to me. Why'd you run? I spoke with the DA. Your case is closed. You have no reason to run."

Easing his head around the corner of one of the machines, Baudin took in the rest of the massive room. At the far end, a conveyor belt sat still. Dark blood stains splotched the concrete floor. The room had seen so much death, it stank permanently of it.

"Henry?"

As quietly as he could, Baudin tiptoed to the door past the conveyor belt. After passing the last machine, he glanced behind him to make sure he was covered. When he turned back around, Peck swung at him with a heavy metal bar.

Baudin ducked just a little too late. The bar hit his arm, which had reflexively come up to guard his head. The impact sent him into one of the machines as Peck lifted the bar and, with a scream, swung it down again.

Baudin leapt out of the way, and the bar dented the metal frame of the machine. He swung around with his pistol, but Peck hid behind the equipment.

"Where you gonna go, Henry?" His heart pounded in his ears. "Where you gonna run to?"

A soft clank came from behind one of the machines, and Baudin caught sight of Henry's boots. He bent down to his knees, took aim, and fired into the first boot. The leather exploded with a small spatter of blood, and Peck yelped.

Baudin rushed him. He smashed the handle of his sidearm into Peck's nose, causing his head to snap back. Baudin kneed him in the groin then swung the weapon again, catching Peck in the mouth. Teeth and blood flew over the machine as Peck lost his footing. He tumbled backward, and Baudin was on him. The handgun crashed into his face over and over, spattering blood up into Baudin's nostrils and mouth. Finally, he stopped. Out of breath and in pain, Baudin sat up. He couldn't tell if Peck was dead.

Suddenly, Peck inhaled a frothy mix of blood and air. He rolled to the side and vomited. Baudin aimed his gun at the man's head. The trigger underneath his finger was so light, a minor tap could have fired the weapon. He held it there for a moment then decided Peck was more valuable alive. Baudin lowered the weapon and returned it to the holster.

"You stupid bastard," Baudin said, leaning down and flipping Peck onto his stomach, "all I wanted was to talk."

"Fuck you," Peck spat.

Baudin slammed him again, causing the man's head to bounce off the cement floor and knocking him out. Before calling it in, Baudin had to lean against one of the machines to catch his breath. He wasn't as young as he used to be, and he wondered how much longer he had in his line of work.

29

Dixon didn't realize Peck had been brought in until Jessop told him. He ran to the back interrogation rooms but didn't see Peck in any of them. He went back out to Jessop, who informed him that Peck was at the hospital and Baudin refused to leave his side.

On the way over to Cheyenne Regional, Dixon scanned the news stations to see if anyone was discussing the case. No one was. Catching a man who'd killed two women in a town as small as Cheyenne should've been big news.

He parked and jogged inside. He showed his badge to the receptionist, who directed him to a room on the second floor. A uniformed officer sat outside the door, reading a magazine.

"He's in there with him, Detective," the uniform said.

"Thanks." Dixon stepped inside the room and shut the door behind him.

Peck lay in a hospital bed with bandages around his face, a strip of medical tape over a large gash in his nose, and both eyes blackened. Baudin sat in a chair across the room. His face, at least one side of it, was swollen and red like a small melon.

"You okay?"

"I'll live."

"What happened?"

"I went to talk, and he ran."

Dixon sat down in a chair on the opposite side of the room. "Did you tell him you were there to arrest him or somethin'?"

"No, nothing. He saw me, froze, and then ran. He just knew he was in deep shit. Animals have a sixth sense about when they're doomed."

"Did you apply for a warrant for his house?"

"Hernandez is on it. We should have it any minute."

Dixon nodded. "You don't need to sit here."

"I wanna be here when he wakes up. He has a concussion."

Dixon looked at Peck. "How long's he been out?"

"Few hours."

"Shit, Ethan. You tellin' me he's in a coma?"

He shrugged. "His choice, not mine."

"And what if he dies? We need an admission."

"We'll find things at his house. I guarantee it. We won't need an admission."

Dixon leaned over and rubbed his forehead. "I'm so sick of this cowboy bullshit. You coulda called him on the phone."

"He knows he's cooked. He woulda run no matter what."

"Well, we won't know that now, will we?"

Baudin's phone buzzed. He looked at it. "They have the warrant. You wanna go search his house or criticize me some more?"

Henry Peck lived in a suburb that could've been on a postcard. Dixon drove them down and realized he'd been out there only once before, on a drug call. The quiet neighborhood, filled with families, was the type of place where the neighbors sat on their porches in the summer and let their children play in the street.

Police tape was up around the home, and the news media had beat them there. Several reporters waited at the edges of the tape, and Dixon knew they would be allowed in at some point. Uniformed officers didn't mind doing favors in exchange for a little bit of airtime or, occasionally, some cash.

Dixon parked farther back, and he and Baudin got out of the car. Baudin put out his cigarette on a fire hydrant then threw it down a sewer drain. They crossed the neighbor's yard and ducked under the police tape. Dixon nodded to one of the uniforms, who nodded back.

Inside, Peck's home appeared as though no one lived there. The furniture consisted of a cot and sleeping bag against the wall and a television on a steel TV stand. No decorations, no memorabilia, and nothing personal adorned the space.

Dixon crossed the living room to the kitchen, which was the same as the living room: nothing. Baudin went straight for the fridge. Dixon glanced that way and saw that the fridge was packed with only meat—either free or stolen samples from the plant.

An officer stepped into the hallway. "You guys should probably have a look at this."

Dixon went down the hallway to find another uniform guarding a dresser drawer. "What we got?"

"Underwear," the uniform said. "Lots of it."

Dixon looked into the open drawers. Women's underwear, everything from thongs to lacey teddies, filled each one. He didn't have any latex gloves, and the forensics unit wasn't out, so he carefully moved the underwear around with a pen he kept in his breast pocket. Searching for something a little more substantive, like jewelry that Peck had taken from his victims, he found nothing but more underwear.

"Could be from victims," Dixon said.

"Could be he likes to wear women's underwear," Baudin said. "Have them run for DNA, I guess."

"You seem disappointed."

"I am. I thought for sure he'd have videos. Someone this vicious—I didn't think a possession would be enough. He'd have to see it. I was sure of it. But I think the underwear's his thing."

"Well, even the pope's wrong sometimes." Dixon looked at the uniform. "Anyone check the basement?"

"No."

Dixon headed down there, and Baudin followed him. The stairs leading down to the unfinished basement were made of pinewood. They creaked and moved with each step, but the lighting in the basement at least let him see where he was going. Peck had placed lights every few feet, even unnecessarily, Dixon thought. *Like he was too frightened to be down here in the dark.* Dixon started on one end, and Baudin took the other. They searched for anything that might give them a window into Henry Peck. But other than a few tools, they found nothing.

Baudin placed his hands on his hips and looked around. "There's something in this house that belongs to those two girls. If we find it, we've got him cold."

Dixon took off his jacket and rolled up his sleeves. "Let's start in the garage."

30

Baudin waited until the forensic investigation team arrived. He wanted everything filmed and photographed before he began tearing it apart. Two techs went through the house, and when Baudin was satisfied every room had been documented, he began taking apart the house.

He cut up the rug, took out the vents and searched inside the ducts, broke open the garbage disposal and various pipes—he left nothing unexamined. In the garage, a sliding door occupied the middle of the ceiling. Baudin found a ladder and climbed up. If it was the stash of Peck's most intimate secrets, he might have set up a trap. He called out, and a uniform came to the door.

"Hold on to the ladder, would you?" Baudin said. "If I'm not out in five minutes, you get my partner and tell him there's a trap up here."

Baudin took the first few steps and, with the muzzle of his sidearm, lifted the door. He slid it over then set it aside. He stuck his head through the hole and looked around. A window provided some light in the space. The room held several boxes and not much else. Baudin climbed up.

There wasn't as much dust or spiderwebs as he thought there should've been, which meant someone cleaned it regularly. Baudin crossed the room, having to duck to avoid hitting his head on the low ceiling, and looked around. He opened the first box.

Photographs of women, clearly taken without their knowledge, filled the first box. Most had been taken through windows into homes and apartments, but some had been taken from inside the homes. Baudin opened the other boxes. They were empty—extra room for more photos.

He picked up a few of the photos and grinned to himself.

Baudin stepped into Peck's hospital room and sat across from him. Peck hadn't woken up yet. Baudin had no doubt the Internal Affairs Division would be down to see him soon and he might even be suspended, but they would have to nail down exactly what happened first. Perhaps there were cameras at Grade A that could back up Baudin's story. He made a mental note to follow up on that.

Baudin sat in the chair a long time, watching Peck. He looked like a man who had worked hard his entire life and had seen little more than work. Baudin had checked his history. Peck's alcoholic mother had raised him after his father ran out on them. When Baudin ran the mother's history, he came up with several convictions for sex solicitation and many more arrests that never led to convictions. She was a prostitute, same as the two girls Peck had killed. Baudin wondered if Peck, once he'd moved from rape to murder, had really been killing his own mother over and over again.

Baudin rose from the chair and stood over Peck's bed. He laid a photo down on his chest: Hannah Smith, nude and in what was clearly Peck's bedroom.

"Gotcha," Baudin said. He left the room and shut the door behind him.

31

The streets were wet from a light rain. Dennis Walk took them slowly, looping around the outskirts of downtown. The kids used to ride up and down State Street, looking for something to do. Eventually, the city outlawed it because the kids occasionally got into fights or pulled over on the street to do drugs. A lot of the kids didn't have money to do anything else and had nowhere to go. Nowadays, they stood on the corners or parked in convenience store parking lots.

Dennis drove by a motel. He'd never slept there, but he'd spent a lot of time in the rooms. In front of the motel, several girls ambled around. They only came out on Fridays and Saturdays and were always in the same spots. He didn't understand why the police weren't there. *Maybe the girls do them, too?*

Dennis knew the girls well. Some of them were runaways, no older than sixteen. A lot of them were just passing through and made the rounds every year through Vegas, LA, Seattle, Salt Lake, Cheyenne, and Phoenix, never staying in one place for too long. And some of them were the regulars, women who had been whoring so long they didn't know what else to do.

He pulled his truck over to the side of the road and waited. They knew who he was and what he liked. They would come to him. He lit a joint and rolled down the window while he smoked. The pot was good, homegrown and fresh, and it made the cabin stink. That didn't matter, though. None of the cops would have done anything if they pulled him over.

Two of the girls, Belle and KP, walked toward him. Neither one of them used their real names and he didn't care. They would do for now.

As he smoked and watched them approach his truck, he scanned the other girls. One on the end was wearing a hat. Her pants were tight, and her shirt exposed her stomach. He didn't recognize her. She was new.

"Hey, Big D," Belle said. "How you been? You lookin' for a party?"

"No, not you." He raised his hand and pointed. "That one."

"Her? She ain't nothin'. Been out here not but a week. You want a real woman."

"You can come, too, but I want her."

She rolled her eyes. "Wait here then."

Belle hurried back and spoke to the girl. She turned around and looked at the truck. The girl's face was angelic. She had alabaster skin and red curly hair that came down over one eye. He couldn't see the color of her eyes, but he hoped they were blue. Slowly, reluctantly, she followed Belle to the truck. She was obviously nervous. That excited him.

"Hi," he said to her.

She smiled shyly. "Hi."

"What's your name?"

"Missy."

"I got a farm, Missy. A lotta pot and coke. You want to come?"

She looked too nervous, as if she had a bad feeling or something.

"These two will come, too. They'll tell ya—I'm good people." He smiled widely. "I just like to have a good time."

She nodded and climbed into the truck.

When all three were in, he pulled away and headed back to his farm.

32

When Dixon stepped into the station on Monday morning, several cheers went up. It had already hit the papers. Forensics had found female DNA on the underwear in Peck's home. The test was just preliminary—a quick run-through in order to obtain further warrants on Peck's locker at work, his car, and his family's house—but the technician had told Dixon he was about eighty percent certain the DNA was female. He could tell him with one hundred percent certainty in two weeks.

Dixon acknowledged the hoots and hollers, and someone had even set coffee and a donut on his desk. Baudin was already there, grinning. Whenever a murder was cleared from the board, much less two, a little celebration was in order.

Several detectives came up and congratulated them, with offers of lunch or drinks after work. Dixon tried not to smile, but he couldn't help it. He hadn't had cause to celebrate in a while. When the other detectives had gone back to their desks, Dixon turned around and saw Baudin watching him.

"What?" Dixon said.

"It's just good to see you happy again. And I got something that'll make you even happier—Peck woke up. We can go see him this afternoon. Looks like we'll get your admission after all."

Dixon and Baudin discussed how they should approach Peck. They decided a honey rather than vinegar approach was best. Peck was unstable and weak. Too much intimidation might shut him down.

After that, Dixon rose and wandered around the detective's bureau, chitchatting with the other detectives. He didn't feel like working, and in fact, the worst part about clearing a homicide from the board was having to pick up a new case and start over.

Jessop was in his office. Since Chief Crest's death, they hadn't had a real conversation. Too many assumptions between them. Dixon assumed that Jessop had known about the chief's proclivities, and Jessop probably assumed Dixon was trying to take him down.

Dixon approached the office and stood at the door. Jessop looked up from his computer but didn't say anything. The two men watched each other for a moment before Jessop said, "That was nice work."

"Thanks." Dixon stepped inside the office and shut the door. He sat down on Jessop's couch. "You and I never talked about the chief."

"What's there to say?"

"I don't know. You tell me."

Jessop leaned back in his chair. "You got somethin' to say, just say it."

"You think that I think you had somethin' to do with it. So let's not bullshit each other."

"And why would I think that?"

"Because it's true."

Jessop sighed. "You want me to apologize for defending my chief? I won't. That's not the way it works. But did I know he was fucking killing people? Of course not. I would've arrested the son of a bitch myself."

Dixon nodded. "I believe you."

"Glad to have your approval. Now you gonna get back to work or what?"

Dixon rose and headed out. Even though few words had been spoken, he'd released a little tension and was glad he'd gone in. He looked over at his desk, where stacks of low-level property crimes needed following up on, and decided he would go out and get a drink.

Before he could leave, another thought hit him. Hesitantly, he took out his cell phone and dialed Hillary's number.

She answered on the second ring. "Hey."

"Hey. I was just seein' if maybe… you and Randy wanted to grab lunch."

"It's ten in the morning, Kyle."

"Breakfast then."

She chuckled. "Yes, we'd both love to."

"I'll come pick you guys up." He hung up and told Baudin he would see him at the hospital later.

At a local diner they had gone to often before they had Randy, Dixon sat across from his wife and listened to all the gossip she had built up over the last eight months. Someone at church had been arrested for marijuana possession, one of the neighbors had fallen off his roof while putting up Christmas lights and shattered both ankles, and her sister was thinking of adopting.

Dixon listened quietly. He hadn't come to talk. He'd come to listen, to really listen. Baudin had once said that women just wanted to be heard. They just wanted someone to listen, not talk or try to fix their problems.

"I miss you," he said suddenly. "And him. I want to move back in. If you'll have me."

She reached over and put her hand over his. "Of course we'll have you. It's your home, Kyle."

"Then if we're going to do it, we need to talk first." He paused. "Why would you do… that? You knew if I ever found out, it would rip my heart in half, and you did it anyway. I just need to know why."

Tears sprang to her eyes, but she fought them back, turning her face to the window. "I was so lonely. Sometimes it felt like I had no one else to talk to. I would take care of Randy all day and you all night. I needed to be the perfect wife and do everything I could to make you two happy, and it felt like no one was there for me. No one was taking care of me, Kyle. I felt completely alone."

Dixon felt tears on his own cheeks. "You could've come to me. You could've told me what was going on, and we could've fixed it."

She shook her head. "Do you know how many times I tried to talk to you? Your head was stuck in your work. I don't think you realize how much energy it takes out of you. You get home, and you're like a zombie. There's nothing left for us."

"That's unfair. I'm doing this for the both of you, not for me."

"Bullshit. You say that, but that's just not true. You love it. You love the chase, the power. You're doing it for you."

Dixon felt anger in his belly, but instead of exploding, he took a deep breath and calmed himself. The gall of it was too much. She'd gone out and fucked another man, lied about it, and lied about Randy being his—and she had the audacity to say she'd done it because of his behavior.

"Maybe this was a mistake," he said.

"The fact that we're talking, actually talking, rather than yelling at each other tells me it's not."

He exhaled deeply and held her hand, feeling the ridges of her skin, running the tips of his fingers over her veins, sliding down to her palm and up her wrist. He missed her touch and the way she held him. Touch carried a truth words never came close to. He knew from her touch that they still loved each other and that he would be miserable without her.

"We need to go to a counselor," she said. "It'll be a lot of work, but we'll get through this. We just need to find each other again."

He stared out the window with her.

33

Missy had never thought she would be in such a position. As she sat in the cabin of the truck and listened to the man in the driver's seat tell them about pig farming, she wished she were anywhere else. Well, almost anywhere else. She would rather be there than at home with her father.

"You a young one," the man, whom the other girls had told her was named Dennis, said. "How old is you? Sixteen?"

"I'm however old you want me to be."

He grinned. His teeth were so yellow, she couldn't see even a speck of white. "How old is you really?"

"Fifteen."

He nodded and smiled. "I like that."

Missy grinned out of courtesy but wished she'd gone with her gut when it told her not to get into the truck. A lot of the girls out on those corners worked for other people and had to go with anyone who offered them a spot. She didn't have to do that. She worked free and clear, no pimp. Cheyenne wasn't dangerous enough for that—or so she'd been told.

"So where were you before here?" Dennis asked.

"I was in Salt Lake City."

"You move out here or just passin' through?"

"Depends on how much money I make, I guess."

Dennis reached over and laid his hand on her thigh. It sent a cold revulsion through her, but she didn't move it. That's what he was paying for. She'd been with several customers before. They'd been kind and gentle. She had heard from some of the other girls that everyone had a secret and that the only place it came out was in the bedroom. Sometimes the secret was gentle, and sometimes it was violent. She tried to tell the difference in just a few seconds of talking with someone.

The farm was on the outskirts of the county. As he drove, Dennis passed around a joint. The other girls smoked, but Missy didn't want any. Most of the time, she had to be high or drunk to fuck a stranger, but right now, she felt she didn't want to be tanked.

The landscape changed from the city to dry desert as far she could see. Night had fallen, but she could see the dark mountains in the distance. Unlike the mountains they had in Utah, they were maybe more like large hills. She would have liked to go out there, climb them, and sit on top. She could look around the state and see it in a way most people didn't.

The farm was blocked by a large barbed-wire fence, the type that kept cattle in. Dennis stopped the truck at the gate and got out. He stumbled over and opened it then got back in and drove through before getting out to close it again.

The dirt road beyond was rough, as though it had not been driven on a lot. The entire place was overrun with weeds and gnarled trees, and the road was littered with trash. The truck rumbled along the road, and the gate slowly disappeared behind them. Soon, they were surrounded by darkness.

The two other girls weren't paying attention to Missy. She was just competition, and they would do everything they could to make her suffer. Some of the other girls gave her tips and took care of her, but some of them, the ones who had been on street corners too long, only wanted to hurt her.

"So what made you wanna be a whore?" Dennis asked over the din of the stereo, which Belle had turned on.

"Just get to meet interesting people like you, I guess."

His face turned. A serious expression came over him, and he stared at her. "You makin' fun of me?"

"No, I mean it. I woulda never met you if I hadn't been doing this. So I get to meet a lotta people I wouldn't meet otherwise."

He thought for a moment then smiled. "I knew I liked you."

Though she grinned, her heart pounded in her ears. Something was wrong with him. He was slow, but that didn't bother her. Something else was wrong.

The first structure on the property she saw was a barn. It was a classic-looking barn with red paint and white trim, but it was so rundown, it looked like it could fall over at any second. Dennis passed it and drove up farther, past a line of trees and a gravel pit, to a massive farmhouse that was larger than any Missy had seen since being in Wyoming. The house faced an open field that seemed to go all the way into the darkness and disappear.

The girls and Dennis got out, so Missy did, too. She followed them up the road toward the house. The girls were high and hugging each other as Dennis led them to the house. He opened the door, and the girls followed him inside. Belle took off her shoes and flopped onto the couch. Missy could tell she'd been there a lot to be that comfortable, and that thought made her feel a little better.

The inside of the home was as dirty as it could be. Old containers of food and empty beer bottles and cans took up the entire floor. Stuff was written on the walls in pens and crayons. The furniture was covered in cigarette burns and discolored with old spills. And the smell was...

Then Missy saw the first pig. A creature about the size of a small dog wandered around the kitchen. It rooted around the garbage and came away with an old slice of pizza. The smell she had noticed was animal feces, so strong that it burnt her nostrils.

Dennis pulled out a small baggy of an off-white powder, meth, probably. Missy liked pot and coke, but she never touched meth. She didn't like the way it kept her up all night. Sleep was her only escape.

The girls started making out with each other and snorting the meth as Dennis sat down in a chair across from them and watched. Missy slipped away to the kitchen, which was empty except for the pig. The smell was even stronger there, and feces caked the floor in such a thick coat that she couldn't see the linoleum underneath. Covering her nose, she went around the kitchen and to the rooms at the back of the house.

Several sets of stairs leading both down and up were throughout the house. She took one and went upstairs. The upstairs was much cleaner and didn't have the feces everywhere. Missy checked the bedrooms. She'd always been fascinated by how people lived, and looking through the homes of strangers was actually an interesting part of what she did.

In one bedroom, a television was mounted on the wall. She sat down on the unmade bed and looked for a remote. *Maybe I could stay up here the whole time?* Dennis and the other two would be so blitzed they wouldn't really remember what happened. She could just pretend she had been involved in the whole thing. *Maybe even still get paid, too.*

She couldn't find the remote, so she rose and left the room. Going back down the stairs, she could see into the living room. The girls were almost completely nude, and Dennis was still sitting across from them, watching. As quietly as she could, she made her way down and decided to check out the basement. The stairs were carpeted, and the smell wasn't as bad as the first floor. Once down there, she stood in the dark for a moment then decided staying wasn't a good idea. Before she could leave, she saw the flickering light of a television.

A woman sat in front of the TV in a wheelchair. Her gray hair covered her face. Missy cleared her throat, but the woman didn't react.

A game show was on. Missy had seen it before but couldn't name it. A host stood in front of a crowd, talking, but the volume on the TV was turned so low that Missy couldn't hear anything. So she crossed the basement and got closer.

"Hi," she said.

The woman didn't respond.

Missy approached the woman and stood near her. Softly, she placed her hand on the woman's shoulder. The woman didn't move. Her eyes—yellowed, with red pulpy veins that bulged out—were open and staring blankly at the television. And then, slowly, they turned to Missy.

The vision sent an icy chill down her back. The eyes held her with rage. They stared at her the same way they had stared at the TV, but Missy had seen her father's rage up close and knew what it looked like.

Missy took a step back, then another. "Sorry," she mumbled. She turned to leave, and ran into the chest of Dennis Walk. She gasped.

He smiled widely. "You shouldn't be down here. You're a naughty girl. And naughty girls need to be punished."

34

Baudin was sitting on the porch, resisting the urge to smoke, when Keri came to pick up Heather. He sipped brandy and held an unlit cigar between his fingers.

Keri sat next to him when Gina went inside. She nudged him playfully with her shoulder. "You look so sophisticated," she said.

"Thought I'd try it. I've never actually had brandy or a cigar."

"What made you want to?"

"I like trying something new every day."

"Really? Every day?"

He nodded and took another sip before placing the glass down. "Every day. That means in a year, I tried 365 new things in my life. I'm bound to like some of them."

She ran her fingers over the dragon tattoo going down his forearm. "Why a dragon?"

"They're really spiritual creatures."

She giggled. "Seriously? It's not just some macho BS about having the biggest and baddest animal on your arm?"

"No. See, in mythology, they represent the heaven and the earth. They slither on the ground, their belly is connected to the earth, but they can also fly. They're a perfect joining of heaven and earth—a goal people try for but never achieve."

"Is that what you're trying for? A perfect joining of heaven and earth?"

He shrugged. "Like I said, it's a goal everyone tries for but never achieves."

Gina shouted, "Mom, let's go."

"Duty calls," Keri said. "How about we meet up this weekend and take the girls somewhere educational for a change?"

"I think your idea of education and mine might be different."

She grinned. "Heather told me the other day that 9/11 was perpetrated by our own government as an excuse to go to war. I doubt she got that on her own. I'm perfectly okay with differing points of view."

He dumped his brandy into the bushes by the porch. "Don't know why anybody would like that. Tastes like gasoline."

She gave him a peck on the cheek. "I know you still think about your wife, and I know you haven't been in a relationship since she passed. Heather told me. I also know you change the subject whenever I talk about us. And that's okay. I understand everyone heals at their own pace. But if you wait too long, I may not be around when you're ready, and we both could've had something really great."

With that, she headed back to her car, leaving Baudin staring at her. She was right. He was still wrapped up in his wife. A woman who'd been dead for years ruled his life as though she were standing right next to him. The truth was, though, that he didn't know what to do about it.

Baudin went inside the house and had a beer to kill time. When afternoon rolled around, he texted Dixon and said he was heading to the hospital. Baudin got into his car and waved to his neighbor on the south side, an elderly man who had fought in World War II. Baudin had asked him about it once—all he'd said was that he was eighteen years old when he went over, and after one year, he came back being seventy years old. They hadn't talked about it again.

The hospital wasn't far, and Baudin drove with his window down. Sometimes, the city appeared to be growing too quickly, and sometimes, he couldn't believe what a small place it really was. He believed that all cities were ultimately the same: places where humanity was crammed in and told to suppress their true behaviors. Still, those behaviors came out in other ways when no one was watching.

In the parking lot of Cheyenne Regional, Baudin lit a cigarette. He smoked it on the walk to the door and put it out before stuffing it into a garbage can. The hospital was busy, at least busier than he'd seen it in the afternoons before, and he went straight to Peck's room. He wanted a minute with him before Dixon got there.

Peck lay in the hospital bed, staring at a television mounted on the wall. He looked horrible: pale and dehydrated. The IV connected to his arm was giving him fluids, but his lips had already started to crack and peel. Baudin turned off the TV then pulled a chair next to the bed.

"You didn't need to run. I just wanted to talk. You could've stonewalled me, and I wouldn't have had anything. Now I got warrants for your house, your parents' house, your car, and your locker. Whatever you're hiding, I'm gonna find it."

Peck didn't say anything at first. His eyelids just dropped down then suddenly opened again. He was clearly on some sort of pain medication, and Baudin was glad for it. He took out his digital recorder and turned it on but didn't let Peck see it. If he did get a confession, Baudin would edit in himself reading Peck his Miranda rights and informing him of the recording.

"You're going to die, Henry. They're going to stick you in the gas chamber for this. See, lethal injection is really expensive, and some states prefer to just strap you into a chair and let you breathe a six-dollar can of hydrogen cyanide. People think you just peacefully fall asleep, but that's not what happens. You'll foam at the mouth, and it'll feel like you're being crushed in a vice. Then your lungs will burst, and you'll suffocate. And the last face you're gonna see is mine. I'm gonna be right there, staring at you while you die, Henry—along with your parents. Can you imagine the look on their faces? As though you weren't a big enough disappointment, now you're gonna make them watch you die."

Peck's face contorted. His eyes closed, and a frown crept onto his lips. "Stop," he said pathetically. "Please stop."

Baudin leaned forward. He had him now. He was just as weak as Baudin had thought he was. Like a shark smelling blood in the water, Baudin circled closer.

"You believe in God, Henry? I never did. Hocus-pocus is beyond me. A truly evolved person leaves fairy tales in childhood. We're the next step in human evolution. The rational being. Reason is our only tool, and emotions are just a method of enjoying life, nothing else. But I still wonder sometimes. I had this foster dad, Jordan, who told me a story." Baudin took out a cigarette and lit it. "He told me that he was at the cemetery once, visiting his mother. He was sitting by her grave, and a funeral was going on up a ways. He usually hung out for a while when he visited on her birthday. He heard something behind him, and when he glanced over, a man was standing there. Just a tall white dude in a suit, staring at him. Didn't say anything, just stood there and stared at him. Jordan tried to talk to him, but he just turned around and wandered away.

"Jordan sat there a bit more, and then he got up to leave. He had to pass the funeral to get to his car. A picture of the deceased was next to the casket. It was the man that was standing behind Jordan. Freaked him the fuck out, Henry. So much that he had to see inside the casket. He waited until the speakers were done and then talked one of them into opening the lid before they buried it. Just a little. He saw the dude inside. Right there. A corpse."

Henry looked at him but didn't say anything.

"Them girls you killed, how many of them are gonna be waiting for you, Henry? How many ghouls you got following you around right now?"

Peck began to cry. He looked like a child who hadn't gotten his way. It was pathetic, and it sickened Baudin.

"I didn't kill anybody," Peck said.

"We got the panties, Henry. We got the panties, and they're gonna match the DNA to Hannah and Shelly."

"No, I steal those. I just steal them. That's all. I ain't never killed no one."

"I don't believe you."

Peck wailed as though he'd just been punched in the gut. "I didn't kill anyone."

"Yes, you did. You raped those girls, and then you killed them, Henry. I want the truth now. Tell me the truth."

He shook his head, his body convulsing with the sobs. "I can't rape nobody. I been castrated."

Baudin froze. He didn't say anything for a long time. Finally, he took a puff of cigarette and stood up over Peck. "What do you mean?"

"I got the shot. They give it every month. You can check with my doc."

Baudin tossed the cigarette into an empty cup on the nightstand. "What doc?"

"He's here. You can go ask him. Barry Houris. Upstairs in the next building over. I couldn't get a hard-on if ten girls was sucking on my cock. I ain't raped no one. And I sure as hell ain't killed no one."

Baudin placed his hands on his hips and stared down at the man. He was sobbing, but he was so dehydrated that no tears were coming out. "I'm gonna check with Dr. Houris right fucking now. And if you're lying to me, Henry, you're gonna be in a world of hurt. You understand me?"

"I ain't lyin'."

Baudin stormed out of the room and went to find Dr. Barry Houris.

35

Dixon had a hard time leaving Hillary. They ate breakfast together then took a stroll around Lion's Park, pushing Randy in a stroller. He didn't respond to Baudin's text. Stuck in a hospital room with Henry Peck was the last place he wanted to be. But he could only ignore it for so long before he knew he had to leave.

"I gotta go," he finally said.

"I know. Will you be home for dinner?"

He nodded. "Yes." He kissed her, then in a move that surprised even him, he bent down and kissed Randy on the head.

When he left the park, he still had a knot in his gut. Whether it was from uncertainty at how the relationship would play out or something else, he couldn't tell. All he knew was that the desire to get drunk was back. The urge was so powerful that he pulled over at the first grocery store he saw and bought a twelve pack. He put it in the trunk and took out two bottles.

By the time he arrived at the hospital, he had a decent buzz. He felt better, as if an itch had been scratched. He debated getting another bottle then decided against it solely because Baudin would say something if he were tipsy. Instead, he popped gum into his mouth and headed toward the entrance.

Baudin was sitting outside on a bench, smoking. Dixon stood in front of him. He'd known his partner long enough to know when something was wrong, and something was definitely wrong.

"Don't tell me he slipped back into a coma," Dixon said.

"No, man. It's worse than that."

Dixon sat down next to him. "What?"

"He didn't do it. He's not our guy."

"How do you know?"

"He's been chemically castrated for years. That's how he got paroled so early. They'll release you if you agree to the shots. I spoke with his doctor, and he's been to every one of his appointments since his release."

"That don't mean he didn't kill those girls."

"These were sex killings, Kyle. Castration doesn't just take away your ability to get an erection, it takes away the urge to have sex. They're like kittens. The panties and stuff we found was probably his attempt to still feel manly. I doubt they did anything for him. And he told me he would steal some of them from Laundromats. If it was a true paraphilia, he would need to steal the panties from their homes. And the photos are just pictures he took of prostitutes. He would pay them for their photo and their panties." Baudin took a puff of his cigarette. "Could be lying to me, but I don't think so. He's not our guy. Our guy rapes these women as part of his ritual."

"I don't get how you make these leaps. Forensics told us there isn't enough of the body left to tell if she'd been raped. You have no idea what happened to her. She could've been partying at the plant with Peck, and he pushed her in or she slipped and fell in. We have no idea. All we got is that this guy is a convicted rapist. He's got panties and photographs in his house and even photos of the vics. How you explain that?"

"It's part of his attempt to feel some sort of arousal. He has to get the shots as part of his parole, but he still *wants* to feel some sort of stimulation. Voyeurism and paraphilias are all he's got left."

Dixon shook his head. "No way. Too much of a coincidence."

"Maybe. I don't know. I just got this feeling like he's not our guy."

Dixon exhaled and leaned back on the bench. "So let's just assume—and I'm serious about assuming—let's just assume he's not our guy. Who, then? Walk?"

"I don't know. I think we shoulda visited the son."

"Well, let's go now."

"First, let's get something to eat and get you some coffee. I can smell the booze on your breath."

After a meal at a sandwich shop, Baudin tossed the sandwich wrapper in the trash and got a large water to go. Dixon had been nursing a cup of coffee from Starbucks and had barely taken two sips. Though Dixon wasn't drunk, Baudin didn't want to hit any potential leads with his partner in the state he was.

"I thought you weren't drinking anymore," Baudin said as they headed outside to his car.

"Just felt like a beer."

Baudin got in and started the car. Dixon sat next to him and searched the glove box until he found a pack of gum. He took a piece.

"You seen Hillary?" Baudin asked.

"Spent the night over there last night."

"You going over again?"

He nodded. "I think I'll be moving back."

"That's what you wanted, isn't it?" Baudin pulled out of the parking stall and headed to the road.

"Yeah, man. It's… nice. Just having someone waiting for you to get off work. It's just nice."

Baudin was about to say something, but his cell phone interrupted him. It was Candi. As far as he could remember, she had never once called him in the middle of the day.

"Hello?"

"You need to come over now," she said.

"What is it?"

"I need to talk to you."

"I'm kinda in the middle of something here, Candi. I can come over tonight."

"You're gonna wanna see what I have to show you."

He glanced at Dixon. "Okay. We'll be over."

When Baudin had hung up, Dixon asked, "Who was that?"

"Candi. Sounded important. Need to make a quick stop at her place."

"You shittin' me? We gotta get to that farm and get a feel for Walk's dickweed son."

"It won't take long. She's never asked me to come over in the middle of the day. It's gotta be something huge."

36

The pain gripped her before anything else. Before she knew she was awake, before she remembered where she was or even who she was, there was only pain. Slowly, Missy opened her eyes.

She was in a large room with cement floors. The walls were unpainted wood, and tool benches were set up around her. She glanced up and saw that she was hanging from a hook, with thick ropes wrapped loosely around her wrists. She had always had small wrists, and the ropes weren't bound tightly enough. She knew she needed to get her arms down from over her head, so she began wriggling free.

The rope was coarse and scraped away her skin. Panic was setting in, and she didn't care if all the skin on her hands got scraped off.

Pulling one arm, then the other, she loosened her hands from the knot. Then one hand slipped out completely. She fell to the floor with a thud, and only then did she realize she was naked.

She wondered if she'd been raped, but she couldn't tell. Her head was spinning, and she ran her hands over her skull to see if she'd come away with any blood, but she didn't. A sharp pain burned on the side of her neck, but there was only a small nick there.

Missy looked up. She was in a barn... *his* barn, the barn she had seen on the drive to the house. The inside was massive, and as she took in her surroundings, things started coming back to her. She had seen the old woman with the fury in her grotesque eyes, then Dennis had grabbed her. She'd felt a sharp pain in her neck then blacked out. She didn't know where the other two girls had gone.

Slowly, she got to her feet. Though no one else was nearby, she covered her breasts with her arms. The air was cold, and she began to shiver. She saw a quilt, dirty with grease, on a workbench. She took it and wrapped it around her shoulders. The only thought on her mind was getting out of that barn. She suspected she'd seen something she wasn't supposed to see, but as far as she could remember, the only thing she'd really seen was the old woman.

Missy hurried to the entrance of the barn. Underneath a workbench, several buckets with dribbles of black fluid staining the exteriors were filled with wet goop. She looked around the rest of the barn. Farther back, away from any windows, was only darkness. She turned back to the entrance and tried the door. It was locked. Keeping her urge to scream in check, she ran to the back of the barn, looking for another way out.

The closest she came was a window that had been blacked out with paint. Farther back was just black, and as far she could tell, there were no light switches. Running her hands along the walls, she circled the entire barn. Coming back to the front entrance, she wanted to pound on the door and scream for help, but she didn't know who that would draw. Instead, she went to one of the workbenches and rummaged through the tools.

Underneath a stack of scrap metal, she found a long screwdriver. The tip was thin, and the edges were sharp. She glanced around then ran back to the darkness. She slid down the wall, the screwdriver in her hands, and waited.

37

Baudin stopped in front of Candi's apartment complex. He got out, and Dixon followed him. Farther down the parking lot, a child was standing by himself with a toy in his hand. The child eyed them but said nothing. Baudin smiled at him, and the child ran off around the building.

He knocked, and Candi answered with a cigarette dangling from her mouth. The apartment stank of pot, and Baudin shut the door once Dixon had come in. He went to sit down at her table to talk—then froze in place.

Lying on the table was a small photograph of Chris Stuttle. He was partially decomposed and completely dismembered. Someone had dug him up, laid him out on the dirt, and snapped a photo.

"Where did you get this?" he stammered.

"Someone knocked on my door a couple hours ago, and by the time I got there, it was just this photo sittin' there. It was in an envelope that had your name written on it. It's right here."

Candi handed him an envelope with his name scrawled across it in pen. Baudin set the envelope down and approached the photo. He placed his palms on the table and stared down at the vacant eyes that had nearly rotted away.

Dixon came up behind and mumbled, "Shit. Fuck me."

Baudin went into the kitchen and got a sandwich bag. As carefully as he could, he slid the photo down by the corner and into the sandwich bag, followed by the envelope. He sealed the bag then held it between his fingers for a second. Dixon was pacing, staring down at the carpet, his hands on his hips. He was starting to panic.

"Who is it?" Candi asked.

"No one. We'll take care of it."

"Am I in danger?"

"I don't know. This was for me. But they know that you have a connection to me. Do you have anywhere else you could spend the next couple nights?"

She nodded. "Friend's house, I guess."

Baudin took out some cash and offered it to her.

She declined. "I think I make more than you," she said.

"Just take it. Please."

She took the cash and slipped it into her bra. "What the hell is this all about?"

"Just a blast from the past," Baudin said casually. "Nothing to worry about."

"If it was nothin' to worry about, you wouldn't ask me to spend the night somewhere else."

Baudin looked down at the envelope and photo. "Pack up. I'll drive you."

They dropped Candi off at a friend's home about twenty minutes away. As she was leaving, she leaned in through the driver's-side window and pecked him on the cheek.

"What was that for?" he asked.

"Just for carin'. Most guys wouldn't give a shit about what happened to me."

Baudin looked forward. "I'll swing by and check on you later tonight."

He pulled away, and he and Dixon were silent for long time before they spoke. Baudin didn't feel like driving out to the Walks' farm anymore. He didn't feel like anything. So he pulled over in a grocery store parking lot.

A young mom was walking into the store and talking on her cell phone while her toddler was running through the lot. A driver slammed on the brakes, and the car's horn blared. The mom flipped off the driver.

"How the hell does anyone else know?" Dixon asked.

"Did you tell anyone?"

"What am I, an idiot? You think I'd tell someone I shot my wife's lover?"

"Did you?"

Dixon stared at him. "No, man. No. I didn't tell anyone. Did you?"

Baudin shook his head. "No. Someone followed me out to the desert."

"But how would they know?"

"They must've been watching us that night. Seen something. I think it's Sandoval."

"Why?"

"We hit him up, and then Candi gets that photo? That's not a coincidence, man. It's Sandoval. It's a message to back off."

Dixon exhaled and looked out the window. "We'll run the photo and envelope, but there's no way there's prints on there."

"No. But we don't need prints. We need to know where the paper and envelope came from. Not every store sells every type of paper. Maybe we can track it down that way."

"Well, drop me off at the station. I'll get it over to the SIS to run."

"And what you gonna say it is?"

"They won't ask. I'll tell him it's follow-up to something personal. Those guys know me."

Baudin exhaled and started the car. He headed to the station. For the first time he could remember in months, he felt a cold tightness in his guts. It was fear.

38

Dixon dropped off the envelope and the paper with a man named Richards in the Scientific Investigation Section of the Cheyenne PD. When Dixon walked in, Richards, wearing a lab coat, was hunched over a thin piece of metal. He was gazing at it through protective goggles, and Dixon stood behind him. As far as he could tell, Richards wasn't doing anything but staring at it.

"Richards, I need a favor."

"One sec."

Another moment went by in silence. Then—*bam!*—a flash went off, and sparks flew off the piece of metal. Richards didn't flinch, but the explosion startled Dixon.

"Shit. What was that?"

"Controlled detonation. Just sulphur dioxide. When you burn it on top of metal, it can make any dried blood stains come to the surface."

"It doesn't burn it away?"

"No. It's like a little miracle. It actually hardens the blood, and we can just take a sample."

"What case is this for?"

"No case. Just saw this at a seminar and wanted to try it. Put some deer's blood on there."

Dixon shook his head. "Whatever floats your boat, I guess." He handed him the sandwich bag. "Everything you can tell me about the letter and the envelope."

"What's it for?"

"Personal favor. Off the books."

"Oh, it must be juicy."

"It is, but it's gotta stay between us."

"Nothing I love more than intrigue. I'll have something for you by morning."

"Thanks, man. And don't blow off any fingers."

Dixon left the basement and went to his desk. He still had other cases, though they were so minor, he didn't want to spend more than a few minutes on them. Finding someone who'd broken a car window or stolen a purse that had been left out at a convenience store was almost impossible without witnesses or video anyway.

The only place in the world he wanted to be right now was home. A decision had slowly been percolating in the back of his mind, and it'd taken fruition that morning: he didn't want a paternity test. It was better to live with the possibility that Randy truly was his biological son. In the moments when the pain and anger subsided, he had to admit to himself that it really didn't matter. He would raise him as his own, no matter what.

Driving home quickly on the freeway as the afternoon slowly turned to evening, he put on his sunglasses so that he could glance at the setting sun. The thought of getting drunk before telling her seemed like a good idea, and he knew something was wrong as soon as he had the thought. But he could consider that stuff later. Right now, he wanted to tell her then start moving his things back into his own house.

When he got home, he practically jumped out of the car and headed inside. A neighbor was mowing his lawn, and Dixon waved. The man looked surprised then waved back. Dixon entered the home, a large smile on his face, and the smile went away instantly.

Hillary was sitting at the table, her arms folded. She looked as if she'd been crying, and several used tissues were piled on the table.

"What's wrong? What happened?" he asked, rushing over to her.

And then he saw what was wrong. Lying in front of her on the table was a photo of Chris, the same photo Baudin's hooker had received. Next to it was an envelope with Dixon's name on it. He closed his eyes. *I have to be dreaming. This can't be real.*

"Did you do it?" she asked.

"Why would you think I did this?"

"Don't lie to me, Kyle. Not now. Did you do this?"

Dixon fell into a chair and slumped over. His eyes wouldn't come up to meet hers. Every ounce of his strength had been sucked from his body, and all he could think was that he needed a drink. "Yes," he said softly.

The admission opened a wound. He had made a resolution not to tell anyone. He and Baudin had vowed to take it to their graves. Out of every person on the planet, she was the last one he wanted to know.

Tears streamed down her face. He shook his head at the absurdity of it. She had her head down in her palms and wouldn't look up.

"Hil," he said, reaching for her.

As soon as his fingers touched her, she jumped back, knocking her chair to the floor. "Don't you touch me! You don't get to touch me anymore." She stormed away and slammed the bedroom door.

Dixon could hear her weeping. He got up and went to the door: it was locked. "Hil, I need to talk to you. Hil?"

He tried the door again, as though expecting a different result. Then he went to the kitchen and collapsed into one of the chairs. The photo was identical to Baudin's, but he picked it up anyway then turned it over. He tore it in half and threw it across the table. In a fit of rage, he jumped to his feet and flipped the table. The crash woke the baby, making him cry.

Hillary didn't come out of her bedroom. Dixon leaned against her bedroom door for a moment longer, listening to her cry. Then he left.

39

Baudin tried Heather's cell and got her voicemail, so he swung home to check on her. She wasn't there. He tried Keri's number. She informed him that both girls had gone to a movie, and she was supposed to pick them up in an hour.

"You eaten?" she asked.

"No."

"Come over for dinner."

Baudin didn't hate the idea of a home-cooked meal eaten with a beautiful woman. Usually, when he was younger, when he was confused or frightened, he'd needed to be alone. Solitude gave some men strength, and it destroyed others. It had always given him strength. *Must be getting weak in my later years.*

"Yeah, I'd love to. I have to follow up on something for a case, though. I'll swing by in a couple hours, if that's okay."

As he passed the kitchen table, Baudin picked up the printouts he'd made. They were photos of Roger Walk, Dennis Walk, and Henry Peck. He stared at the picture of Dennis Walk. He had a deformity in his upper lip—a cleft palate almost, but not quite. It caused his lip to curl up. The only picture of Dennis he could find was an old DMV photo. Baudin tucked the photos into a file folder then rushed out the door.

He remembered where he'd dropped Candi off, and he drove thirty miles per hour over the speed limit. He had a feeling that whoever had sent him those photos had something else in store for him and that it wasn't far away.

He was convinced Sandoval was behind the photo. Sandoval—not the mayor or the business magnates who lived up on the hill—ran Cheyenne. He had founded Sigma Mu and was its oldest living member. No one would've dared to send that photo without Sandoval's okay.

But the man seemed impenetrable. He was surrounded by layers of sycophants, and Baudin was still an outsider. He was a transplant from a big city, and all the locals thought the city folks looked down on them. That couldn't have been farther from the truth, though. Baudin saw them as more authentic than the people in the big cities. Most of the people tried to do good and not lie, cheat, or steal. He didn't feel that was a common human trait anymore.

Baudin parked in front of the house and crossed the lawn. The door was open. He poked his head in and saw three women sitting in the living room, watching television. Baudin opened the door and knocked once he was inside the house. Candi smiled and rose from the couch.

"You should keep the door locked," he said.

"No one knows I'm here."

Baudin glanced at the other two women. "I need to show you something." He took the photos out of the file. "Do you recognize any of them?"

Candi looked carefully at each photo. "Just him," she said, pointing to Dennis Walk. "Dennis."

"He's a regular?"

"Oh, yeah. Like every weekend. He picks up one or two girls, and they head up to his farm. Even if he doesn't pick up the girls, his farm's always open for partying. Lots of drugs he doesn't charge anyone for. He's got an inheritance or something, so he doesn't care about money none."

"He ever try to hurt you or any of the other girls?"

"Dennis? No, he's a sweetheart. Real shy. He treats us like family. A lotta the girls even give him freebies."

Baudin stared at the man's photo. "Any girls not come back after goin' with him?"

She shrugged. "I don't know. I don't think so. But there's other places you can pick up whores. We all got our spots."

One of the women in the living room shouted, "I been with him once."

Baudin hurried over to her and showed her the photo. "With him?"

She nodded. "Yeah, Dennis. Up at the farm."

"Did you see or hear anything out of the ordinary? Did he try to hurt you or have any odd requests?"

"They all got odd requests, honey. But no, Dennis was fine. It's his mama that creeps me the fuck out."

"His mom?"

"Yeah, she's, like, in his basement. Scary shit. We ain't allowed to see her, though."

"What kind of things does Dennis request?"

"He likes bondage, the rough stuff. Ties us up sometimes."

"Anything else at his farm seem out of place?"

She shook her head. "No, don't think so. It's a big place, though."

Baudin stared at the photo of Dennis Walk for a moment then stuffed all three photos back into the file. He took out his phone and dialed Dixon's number, but no one answered.

"You doin' okay?" he asked Candi.

"Fine, hon. You take care of yourself. Don't worry about me."

"I'll clear this thing up as fast as I can. I'm sorry."

"Don't be. Shit happens."

Baudin left. He had been looking in the wrong place. He'd been so focused on Peck that he'd completely neglected a man who was addicted to prostitutes. And it was an addiction, as surely as heroin or coke was. Baudin had seen a lot of it in his time with the Special Victims Division of the LAPD. Men got addicted to pornography then made the leap into visiting prostitutes. Once they saw how easy and quick it was, they would frequent them more and more. Then one day, they couldn't go very long without one.

Baudin's cell phone rang. It was a station number. "This is Baudin."

"Detective Baudin," Bill Jessop said on the other end, "I need you to come in right now, please."

As far as Baudin could remember, Jessop had never once used the word *please* with him. "For what?"

"Your partner's here, and I need to speak to both of you. Just get here. Now."

Jessop hung up. Baudin threw the file on the passenger seat and sat in his car, thinking. He wanted to head up to the Walks' farm right away. *How much trouble would I really be in if I just ignored Jessop and saw him tomorrow?*

But he didn't want to go to the farm without Dixon. So he started the car and headed back to the station.

40

Missy sat in the dark for a long time, so long that she began to drift off. Then the sound of the entrance to the barn sliding open woke her. It sounded old, and metal squealed as the door hit the other side. A cold draft blew in. She couldn't hear crickets but saw sunlight come in. She guessed it was early morning.

Footfalls echoed in the barn. The shoes were softer than boots. They came to the center of the room and stood still, then they began to move again. Missy's heart thumped so hard that she thought she might lose her breath. The screwdriver was slick in her sweaty hands. Trying to calm her breathing, she breathed through her mouth as softly as she could. The footfalls grew louder as they approached.

It was too dark to see much more than shadows. But that meant it was too dark for him to see, too. Slowly, the figure came into view.

Missy could feel something rising in her throat. She felt sick, as if she might puke. Her hands were trembling, and she gripped the screwdriver even more tightly. As quietly as she could, she got to her feet.

The figure wasn't far now. Just around the corner. *Please, please, please, please…*

Her mind was a soup of fear and confusion. Nothing but that single word stuck for very long. No one thought could penetrate the cloud that had settled in. But that one word kept coming to her, though she didn't know to whom she was saying it. *Please, please, please, please…*

The figure was right there, right next to her. She could hear his breathing. Missy closed her eyes, said a prayer, then jumped out, screaming. She stabbed at the shadow and completely missed. Then she heard another sound—more screaming.

She thought it was the echoes of her own screaming, but the shadow had jumped back, and she could see the outline of Belle. The other woman was nude, too.

"She's dead," Belle said, in a stupor. "She's dead. Jenny's dead."

"We need to go."

"She just died right there. They made me watch. She's dead."

Missy pulled her out near the light of the open door and could see her eyes were glazed over. Her head bobbed slightly back and forth.

"We need to go, Belle. Right now."

"They made me watch."

Missy took her hand and pulled her out of the barn. The sky was lightening. Holding Belle's hand tightly, Missy ran. She didn't slow down. The only thing keeping her from a full sprint was Belle.

They passed the truck, and she considered seeing if the keys were in there. Instead she decided to run for it—to run and not stop running.

The rough dirt road hurt her feet. It was hard and pebbly. Behind her, she heard shouting, but she didn't look back. A moment later, the rumble of the truck engine started, and she heard the tires kick up dirt.

"Don't stop!" Missy shouted.

41

Baudin got to the station well into the evening. Heather would be sleeping over at Keri's house. Baudin felt bad about imposing on her all the time, but Keri had said she loved the girl, and it made Gina happy. He didn't know if she was being nice or if that was true, but Keri did seem lonely. Maybe the sound of girls running around the house alleviated some of that loneliness.

The station was nearly empty, and the detective bureau was completely empty. The only light on was in Jessop's office. Baudin headed there and found Dixon sitting on the couch. His eyes were rimmed with red, and even from the doorway, Baudin could smell the booze on him. He could guess what the meeting was about. Dixon had been drunk on duty, and Jessop wanted to nail him for it.

"Bill," Baudin said as placatingly as he could, "you should know that Kyle went through about the worst thing a husband and father could go through. He did the best he could with what—"

Baudin spotted the photograph of Chris, his dismembered body loosely thrown together like some grotesque jigsaw puzzle, on Jessop's desk. His heart stopped.

"I got this in the mail," Jessop said, "along with a cartridge retrieved from the body. One cartridge, from Kyle's gun."

"Allegedly from Kyle's gun," Baudin said. There was no way a ballistics match had been made that fast.

"Kyle told me what happened."

Shit.

"What did he say happened?" Baudin asked.

"He said he shot the fucker and then buried him out in the desert. That true?"

Baudin looked at Dixon, who wouldn't meet his gaze. "I want my union rep. So does Kyle."

"He already confessed, dipshit."

"Get us our reps."

"I will. But first, you're gonna do something, Detective Baudin. You're gonna place your partner under arrest, read him his rights, and take him down to the holding cells."

"The fuck I will."

"It's fine." Dixon stood up. He nearly fell over then caught himself against the wall. "It's fine."

"Kyle, shut the fuck up, man."

"No, I'm sick of lying. I can't handle it anymore. I'm sick of it. I just want it to be done."

"Kyle, you better—"

"It's over, Ethan." He held out his wrists.

Baudin looked at Jessop, who had a smirk on his face. *He's been waiting for this. Wanting something like this.* Baudin's lip curled, and he considered grabbing something off the desk and whacking Jessop in the face with it.

"Ethan, just do it, man. I'm fine."

Baudin exhaled loudly. He took out his cuffs and put them on his partner's wrists. "You have the right to remain silent…"

42

Baudin led Dixon to the cells. The holding cells of any station were maintained just enough to avoid lawsuits. They were places where people who couldn't be stuck anywhere else went to sober up or await transfer to the metro jail. Cold, dirty cement walls and metal doors that slid closed with a loud bang let the inmates know they weren't going anywhere.

Baudin took off Dixon's cuffs and sat next to him on a bench circling the cell.

"What did you say?" Baudin asked.

"He brought me into the office and confronted me. I told him everything. Everything except your part. I said I did everything."

"Why?"

Dixon put his face into his palms and sobbed. Baudin placed a hand on his back and let him finish. When he was done, Dixon sat up and leaned back against the wall, his cheeks flushed from dehydration and alcohol.

"They sent one to Hillary, too. She asked me if I did it. I tried to deny it, but she could just tell. She could always tell."

Baudin leaned forward on his thighs, staring at the dirty floor. "We're in a world of hurt, man. This isn't good. You'll get life in prison."

"I don't care."

"You will when you sober up." Baudin took in a deep breath and rose. "I'll figure a way out of this. For now, you don't talk to anyone but our union rep, okay? Kyle, okay?"

"Okay."

"No one. Not even Hillary."

"Okay. I won't talk. For you." He paused. "You're the best friend I ever had, Ethan."

He snorted. "Don't get all pussy on me now." He put his hand on Dixon's shoulder. "Keep your head up. I'll get us out of this."

With that, he left, letting the door slam shut behind him. Baudin walked over to the night shift desk and told the guard there, "You get him whatever he needs. He's one of us."

"I know. I'll take care of him."

Heading to the stairs, Baudin caught a glimpse of his partner inside the cell. He had his face in his hands again and was crying.

Baudin marched straight into Jessop's office. "You didn't have to do that."

"He murdered someone. You know how that's gonna play out? Especially after all that shit with Crest?"

"We could've handled this privately. You want him marched in front of the cameras in handcuffs."

Jessop leaned back, a smile on his face. "So what if I do? Revenge is revenge, ain't it?"

Baudin shook his head. "No. It just escalates it for everyone. You're wrong about this."

"Shit. We'll see, won't we?"

Baudin stomped out of the detective bureau and sat in his car. He breathed silently for a moment then slammed his fist into the steering wheel. He punched it over and over, until his knuckles ached and someone came out of the station in response to the horn. Baudin didn't say anything to him. He just started the car and peeled away.

A bar he'd found some months back sat next to a pool hall at an intersection downtown. Baudin went inside and ordered a whiskey. He drank it down then finished two more before he finally ordered a beer. His mind was buzzing. His thoughts swirled over and over to that night that he'd disposed of Chris's body. *How could I have been followed?* He'd waited until the middle of the night and left for the desert. He didn't remember any taillights. *I would've noticed something like that.* The only way someone could've been there was if a pro had been following him—or Chris.

Baudin drank his beer in a couple of gulps and stared at the froth in the bottom of the mug. He watched the bubbles pop and fizzle. He didn't know what to do. His partner would go down. Baudin could step up and tell them he'd done it all, but he would be leaving Heather alone. Randy at least had his mother. *This can't be it. There has to be a way out of this.*

A ruckus came from the other side of the bar, then two men exploded into a brawl. One grabbed a stool and swung it as if he were a medieval warrior with a battleax. The other one let the stool smash into him and then tackled the warrior. They both hit the floor in a flurry of fists and blood. Baudin watched the brawl passively. It didn't even dawn on him until he felt his sidearm strapped to his hip that he was a cop and bound to stop the fight.

Fuck that. He wasn't going to be a cop much longer. He knew he was going down just like Dixon was.

One of the men reached back and slammed both fists down into the warrior's face like an ape smashing a walnut. The warrior went limp, twitched a few times, then went limp again. The other man said, "Oh, shit," and was out the door in under a couple of seconds, no doubt thinking he'd killed the man.

Baudin rose to check on him, but he was in no condition to do anyone any good. The bartender was calling in an ambulance anyway. As he was debating what to do, Baudin's cell phone rang. The number belonged to the station, probably his union rep or an IAD detective wanting to interview him about Christopher Stuttle's death. Baudin turned off his phone.

He ordered another beer, laid his head down on the bar, and closed his eyes.

43

Dixon stared at the floor. It was covered in dead cockroaches. A particularly large one was crawling over the others slowly, half his guts hanging out after being stepped on... then it stopped. It was the last one of them that was alive.

The guard, a man Dixon knew, came over. "You need anything, Detective? Food? Gatorade or somethin'?"

"No, thank you, Tyler. I'm good. Just a blanket if you don't mind."

"Be back in a jiff."

Dixon lay down on the bench. In the last two hours, the drunkenness had faded, leaving only shame and fear. An icy, dead fear sat in his gut as though he'd eaten a rock. He'd confessed to Jessop and Hillary. Everything was out in the open now. Charges would soon be filed, then the media shitstorm would begin. A homicide detective who'd committed a homicide wasn't going to just be let go or get a small blurb on some blog then be forgotten. His family and friends would be hounded for interviews for weeks to come. Every aspect of his life and career would be torn apart to find some kernel the media could use to try to explain his behavior.

He heard footsteps in the hall and looked up as his door opened, expecting Tyler to be there with the blanket. Instead, he saw a man in a suit. Dixon didn't recognize the man at first, not until he sat down next to him and sighed.

"Quite a pickle, ain't it?" Sandoval said.

Dixon noticed that, though it was probably late at night, Sandoval was dressed for the courtroom. His shoes were shiny, and his tie was knotted firmly at his throat.

Dixon looked away. "You can gloat later. I just want to be alone right now."

"I don't want to gloat, Detective. I never did. You're one of us. One of the people fighting on the streets to have some semblance of a normal life for the people out there. You see it, I know you do. Every time you drive by someone's house and see their kids playing outside, it hits you—you're different. You see the world differently—much closer to the way it actually is than the way you'd like it to be. You're one of the few people who've seen the abyss and know what we really are. And it terrifies you that no one else sees it." He looked off. "I've seen it, too, Detective Dixon. I know what's out there. The world is a choice between the lesser of two evils. I am the lesser of the two you have before you."

Dixon swallowed. "What do you want?"

"I want something simple: loyalty. It's such a rare gift in a man. I've lived on this earth now sixty-eight and a half years, and do you know I can count the number of loyal—truly loyal—men I've encountered on one hand?"

Dixon stared at him. "He was right about you. You sent those photos."

He grinned. "By *he*, I assume you mean Detective Baudin, and yes, he is a clever one." He grimaced. "I do wish I could get loyalty from him, but he's not like us, Kyle. He's not country folk. We look out for our own. We always have. So I'm asking you: will you look out for me?" He placed his hand on Dixon's thigh gently then rose. "Sleep on it. I don't want an answer while you're inebriated. If yes, a whole new world of opportunity is going to open up for you. Things you couldn't believe. If no, well…" He glanced around the cell. "Then I hope you like your accommodations. Because you will never get out of a prison cell again."

As Dixon listened to Sandoval's footsteps disappear in the hall, he had never felt so alone.

Another couple of hours passed, and Dixon slept. He woke to the sound of his door opening again and saw that a blanket had been laid on top of him, though he didn't remember anyone doing that.

Hillary walked in. Her face was puffy, and her eyes were red. She was wearing sweats, and her hair was a mess, but she had never looked so beautiful to him. She sat down near his feet and played with her fingers. Dixon didn't speak. When he sat up and took her hand, she didn't fight him.

"Do you want to know the worst part?" she said. "I lashed out at you, but I know it's my fault. This whole thing is my fault. I mean, what did I think would happen?" She paused. "And now Chris is dead. Chris is dead because of me."

Dixon felt like crying, too, but he didn't have it in him. He felt utterly numb, as though he would never feel anything again. He wanted to say something comforting to his wife, but nothing came.

"What's going to happen to you?" she asked after a long cry.

"I'm going to prison."

"For how long?"

"I would guess at least ten to twenty years, maybe more. I could be gone the rest of my life, depending on what the DA charges me with." He said it so matter-of-factly, it surprised even him. The prison sentence was a foregone conclusion, something he'd already accepted.

She shook her head. "No. No, please. I can't lose you. Not like that. Not like that." Her head fell into his chest, and she began to cry again.

He wrapped his arm around her and pressed her body against his. In that moment, Dixon knew what his life had been about and where he had gone wrong. With her in his arms, he knew that he would do absolutely anything for his family. No matter what pain Hillary put him through, no matter how degraded he felt, he would do anything to be with her.

And that, he knew, was going to be his death.

44

Baudin, despite his bravado, didn't even have the strength to drink. Drinking wasn't madness: men drank to escape so they could prevent madness. But he didn't want to prevent that right now. Maybe the insane had it figured out. Maybe the proper response to this insanity was insanity.

He rose from the barstool and left two twenties on the bar. Paramedics had carted off the warrior. He wasn't dead, but they thought he'd suffered a concussion. An officer had come to speak to Baudin, but he'd showed him his badge and told him to piss off.

Outside, the air was cool, much cooler than it should've been. A storm was coming. Baudin had a back injury from his time as a beat cop in LA, and whenever it was about to storm, the injury flared up. He leaned against his car in the dark and smoked. Options had to be considered. He could grab Heather and leave. Right now. Tonight. *But where would we go?* The DA's Office would see it as running and issue a felony warrant. They would extradite him anywhere he went in the United States.

Another option was to kill whoever was responsible. Ultimately, he didn't know who that was, but his money was on Sandoval. He suspected someone had been following him and Dixon, and that person had seen the murder then followed Baudin out to the desert. If Baudin killed Sandoval, the scrutiny might go away. Then again, Dixon had just confessed. The state had a case regardless of whether Sandoval or someone else was at the helm.

The final option was to suck it up and take whatever came. That seemed the worst of the three because that would mean giving up control. Rather than being proactive, he would have to fight off whatever was thrown at him.

As he thought, his cell phone rang. It was Keri.

"Hey," he said.

"The girls are asleep. Just thought you'd want a check-in."

"I appreciate it. Thanks. I should've called. My mind's elsewhere right now."

"Work, huh?"

"You could say that. I just got a shit of a decision, and I don't know which way to turn."

"One of those. I hate those."

"Me, too."

She sighed. "So, I'm here. Talk to me."

"I'm not the type to dump my problems on other people."

"Other people? Come on, Ethan. I'm sick of this bullshit. We're dating. You're as close to a boyfriend as I've had in years, and I'm guessing you haven't even held another woman's hand since your wife passed."

He scratched an itch on his forehead with his thumb then lit another cigarette. "I like you, Keri. I really do. But you don't want to be involved in the shitstorm that is my life."

"I know about the shitstorm. I knew about it from Heather before the day I met you. So don't give me that 'It's not you; it's me.' I'm in, Ethan. You say the word, and I'm in."

He grinned. He appreciated her tenacity. His wife had been the same way. "There's some bad things I've done. And I'm not sure how to fix it. Sometimes, it feels like the darkness just gets to win. Like the game is rigged from the beginning."

"If that were true, there'd be no point to all this. And whether there's a point to this or not, you have to believe there is."

"Why?"

"Because you make your own life. You choose what you want your life to mean. I learned that pretty quick after the divorce. I had nothing and no one and a daughter that was relying completely on me to provide for her. So I could've sat around and thought the universe was out to get me, or I could fight. And I chose to fight. For her. You have Heather. Are you gonna lay down, or are you gonna fight for her?"

Baudin blew out a puff of smoke. He thought of his daughter. When she was young, she couldn't pronounce the letter *D* and had called him "Bab." It made him chuckle every time. Then one day, she could say Dad, and then Ethan, and she began to understand the world around her. Pretty soon, she went from missing him to forgetting he was around. And it didn't matter. His love for her never waned. Even when she was an old woman, he wouldn't love her any less. She was the reason he was alive, the reason he got up in the darkness every morning and decided that he was going to bring just a little more light to the world. For her. It'd always been for her.

He felt the warmth of tears on his cheek and wiped them away. "Thank you," he said softly.

"Come over. Come over and spend the night with me."

He nodded, though no one was around. "I will." His other line beeped. He pulled the phone away from his cheek and saw that the call was from Dixon's cell phone. "I gotta take this. I'll be over as soon as I can."

"I'll be waiting."

Baudin switched lines. "This is Baudin."

"It's me," Dixon said.

"They gave you your phone, huh?"

"No. I'm out."

Baudin hesitated, his mind racing. "How?"

"The DA is declining to file charges."

"That quick?"

"Yeah."

Baudin tossed his cigarette. "He's playing with us, man. This is a game. He wanted to show us what he could do if he wanted to, and now he's not gonna file. It's all a game."

Dixon was silent for a moment. "We need to hit Walk up tonight."

"Why?"

"Because I know he's our guy."

"How do you know that?"

"I just do. And it has to be tonight." He paused. "I won't be able to do it tomorrow."

"What's all this cryptic shit, Kyle? What's going on?"

"Look, we gotta hit Walk up tonight. Now. Like right now."

Baudin watched a car pull away from the bar. "Okay. I'm in. You still at the station?"

"Yeah."

"Gimme ten."

45

Dixon walked out of the station as Baudin parked at the curb. Baudin could see his gun and shield while he slung on his jacket. Something wasn't sitting right with Baudin. They had Dixon cold for murder, and he was walking out of the station still a cop. *Would Sandoval really go this far just to fuck with us?* Baudin decided he would. The message was clear: back off, or I'll take everything.

Baudin stepped out of the car and lit a cigarette. He went to the trunk and popped it. Dixon came over, and they pulled out the Kevlar vests and began strapping them on. Dixon seemed distant. He wouldn't look Baudin in the eyes, and though he still stank of alcohol, he had sobered up.

"You sure you wanna do this tonight?" Baudin asked.

He nodded. "Has to be tonight."

"Without backup?"

"Just us. No one else."

"You know this is nuts, right? He could have an arsenal up there waiting for us."

Dixon took a shotgun from the trunk. "You wanna do this or not?"

Baudin stared at him. Something had changed, something unseen that Dixon didn't want to share. "Yeah, man. I wanna do this. I wanna make sure that piece of shit never kills another girl again. We make the world a little better. That's our job, whether the law is on our side or not. But I'm surprised you see it."

"Just took some nudging is all."

Baudin took a step toward him. "I'll fight the darkness every day for my daughter. What are you fighting for, Kyle?"

Dixon held his gaze. Then he stepped around him and opened the passenger-side door. "Let's go."

As they drove and the night dwindled to the coming day, Baudin's unease grew. He knew for certain something was wrong. Dixon had always wanted backup, no matter where they went. The fact that he wanted them alone meant he wanted a certain outcome.

"What happened in there, Kyle? Something did. I'm fine going in there and doing what I think you want to do. But I want to know why."

Dixon was silent for a few seconds. "Sandoval came and saw me."

"What did he say?"

"He said Walk was the guy we're lookin' for."

"What else?"

Dixon glanced to him. "He was havin' us followed. That's how they found Chris. One of the investigators from the DA's office was just down the street when I ran in there and shot him. He just waited until you came out and followed you."

"And Sandoval just gave you this information out of the goodness of his heart?"

"He got me out of a life sentence. I don't give a shit why."

The darkness turned to a light gray as they approached the farm. They came to a gate up a dirt road, where Dixon got out and swung the gate open. Baudin drove through then waited for him. Dixon even seemed to move differently. He had a swagger to him. He'd come to a decision about something.

They drove up the road another five or ten minutes, then Baudin saw something in the distance—figures running toward the car.

"Shit." He jumped out of the car and pointed his sidearm.

Dixon did the same. As the figures neared, Baudin could hear them. They were nude and screaming. Two women.

"What the shit..."

Baudin lowered the gun but didn't holster it as he approached. One of the women was covered in blood. She seemed to be following the other one. Baudin ran up just as a truck came barreling toward them. The pickup swung wide then bolted straight for Baudin.

He fired, getting off three rounds. Two went into the truck, and it swerved, cutting between the women and Baudin. The man grabbed the first woman, a younger one, and held her in the driver's-side window like a shield before peeling off and back down the way he came. Baudin took aim but didn't fire for fear of hitting the girl.

He ran to the second woman, Dixon behind him.

"Was that Walk?"

"They... they made me watch while they killed her."

"Who's 'they'? How many of them are there up there?"

The woman was loopy, barely able to stand, much less talk. Baudin figured she'd been drugged. He quickly led her back to the car and put her in the backseat. He took out his cell phone.

Dixon said, "No."

"No what? She needs an ambulance."

"You're not calling it in. This is us and him."

Baudin stared at his partner for a second then tucked the phone back into his pocket. He turned to the woman. "Stay here."

He grabbed another pistol out of the trunk and tucked it into his ankle holster before the two of them started jogging up the road toward the farm.

46

The road narrowed, and up ahead was a barn. Thick white pine trees filled the landscape before them as the sun began its slow ascent in the sky. A breeze was blowing, and Baudin listened to the rustle of the leaves as they got closer.

They stopped near the barn. The truck was parked up the road, next to a house. Baudin and Dixon each took a spot against the barn on either side of the door. Baudin nodded, and Dixon opened the door for Baudin to rush in.

He swept right and left, but it was dark. Leaning down on one knee, Baudin immediately smelled the scent of blood. It was distinct. He rose and moved to the side of the door as Dixon came in, shotgun at his shoulder.

Baudin slid along the wall, looking for a light switch. He felt one near a door and flipped it, turning on a single, swinging lightbulb in the center of the barn. Next to the bulb were chains and hooks. He lowered his weapon and stood underneath the hooks.

"I think he's in the house," Dixon said.

Baudin ran his eyes along the wall. Underneath a workbench was a series of buckets. He went to it and pulled out the first one.

"What is it?" Dixon asked.

Baudin kicked it over, spilling the black contents, which oozed along the floor like maple syrup. Left inside the bucket were two hands and a head. The face had rotted away, leaving only a skull and dark black hair.

Baudin lifted his weapon and searched the rest of the barn. In a room in the back, they found a locked door. Baudin lifted his leg and bashed at the wood until it splintered.

Dixon went in first and swept the room. "Holy shit," he said.

Laid out on several metal tables were the remains of girls—two full corpses and another one that was in the beginning stages of being cut. Meat cleavers and bone saws lay on a workbench in the corner. A butcher's smock hung against the door.

"Who the hell have we been chasing?" Dixon asked.

A scream came from the house. The two of them looked at each other then sprinted out of the barn and toward the house. Dixon ran around back, and Baudin took the front. Usually, he liked working alone, but he would've really appreciated having SWAT do the entry. He debated calling it in now without Dixon's knowledge—then he heard a shotgun blast.

He rushed into the house. The place looked like a garbage dump. His every step knocked aside cans, wrappers, and other trash. The smell burned his nostrils. In the kitchen, he found a thick layer of what he thought was dirt, but as he got closer, he saw it was manure.

He rushed through the kitchen and to the back of the house, where he saw Dixon, who had blood spatter on his pants. On the floor in front of him lay a pig with a hole the size of a baseball in his head. Dixon was breathing hard, and the two men watched each other for a second before Baudin looked over at the hallway leading into the rest of the house.

"You take the upstairs," Baudin said.

When Dixon had rushed up the steps, Baudin took the first set going down. The house was huge and had four different staircases: two going up and two going down. Baudin took the stairs gingerly, listening intently for any sounds.

At the doorway, he looked left then scanned around to the right. Little light penetrated down there, and he flipped a switch, which turned on the track lighting. Off to the side, in another room, he heard canned laughter. He had to take a few steps in that direction then peeked around a corner to see a wheelchair in front of a television set. The volume was turned so low, he could hardly hear it.

Baudin heard footsteps behind him, and Dixon came down. He let the shotgun hang as he looked around. "Upstairs is clear. The other stairs leading down go to a storage room. There's no one here."

"He must've taken off on foot. Grab the car. I'll run after."

Dixon took off up the stairs, and Baudin was about to leave when he noticed a closet across the room. One of the sliding doors was open maybe three inches. He held his firearm low and carefully went over there. Using two fingers, he slid the closet door open a crack. Nothing was inside but boxes of old shoes and clothes. As he stepped away, he heard a shriek. Then fire shot through him.

An old woman had thrust the blade of a knife into his hip. He slammed his elbow into her face, and she stumbled back. Blood spurted from her mouth, and Baudin ripped the knife out of his flesh then threw it against the wall.

The woman shrieked and ran for him again, her eyes wild like an animal's. He lifted his weapon and fired two rounds. Both slammed into her chest. The woman flew onto her back. A sucking sound came from her chest where the blood sputtered and flowed.

The pain in his hip burned, and he reached down and pressed his hand to the wound. Then the other side of the closet door opened, and Dennis Walk stabbed a metal hook into his back. Baudin screamed and Dennis ripped the hook out, along with a slab of flesh.

Baudin spun to get his weapon up, and Dennis tackled him. The man was bigger and stronger than Baudin was. Dennis lifted the hook again and swung down. The metal pierced Baudin's shoulder then tore downward as Dennis pulled on it. Baudin grabbed the hook with one hand to prevent it from tearing any farther down. His hand holding the gun was pinned beneath Dennis's girth.

Baudin had to make a choice. The hook would tear right through his chest. He dropped the gun and wrapped his arm around Dennis's neck. Both men grunted like animals. He pulled Dennis against his chest, preventing him from having the leverage to tear out anything else with the hook. Behind Dennis in the closet, the young girl lay naked, not moving. Despite the pain, despite the struggle and burning in his arms from keeping Dennis against him, Baudin couldn't help but think that the girl wasn't that much older than Heather was.

Dennis got one hand loose, and the hook dug deep enough to strike bone. Baudin thought he would pass out. He let go of Dennis's neck and grabbed his gun. Dennis grabbed the gun, too. The hook began to pull out of his flesh as Dennis focused on the gun.

Baudin thought of Heather and what she would do if he died there. Who she would become flashed in front of him—a woman who could never form relationships or have a connection because she'd lost both parents at such a young age. He wouldn't let that happen. He would live for her.

Baudin let go of the gun, and Dennis grabbed it with both hands. Ripping the hook out with one hand in an overwhelming burst of pain, Baudin swung with a backhand. The hook entered Dennis's neck as he tried to lift the gun. Baudin spun, gripping the hook tightly. The metal tore across Dennis's throat.

Blood poured out as though a balloon had burst. It rained down over Baudin, and he panicked as it got into his mouth and eyes. He crawled away, using his uninjured arm to pull himself out from underneath Dennis.

The gun fell to the floor. Wet, gurgling sounds came from Dennis as he flopped like a dying fish. Convulsing, he pressed his hands against his throat, trying to staunch the flow of blood that wouldn't slow. Baudin watched him die.

Then he got the gun and put two rounds into Dennis Walk's head. Another sound startled him, and he turned. The girl was still alive. He took out his cell phone and dialed 9-1-1.

47

The next morning, Baudin was still in the hospital. They had stitched him up and put him on antibiotics, but the knife had missed all his major organs. The hook had left large wounds that would need surgery, and infection was the doctors' main concern now.

While the nurse went off to care for other patients, Baudin snuck outside and lit a cigarette. He stood next to a bench in front of the hospital and smoked. Dixon rolled up, got out of his car, and approached Baudin. He sat down on the bench, and Baudin sat next to him.

"That was his mother that attacked you," Dixon said. "SIS and the FBI are up there right now."

"Who called the feds?"

"Jessop did. He thought this was too big for us."

"Bullshit. He didn't want the work. Easier to let them take it now that Walk's dead."

Dixon didn't say anything for a moment. "They think they found the remains of at least thirty girls. I knew a few of them from my beat cop days. Streetwalkers."

Baudin nodded. "They're easy to get up to the farm."

"They think he was hiding the... meat, I guess you'd call it, by putting the bodies in grinders at Grade A. It was his dad's business, and he had all the codes to get in after hours. They think the machine burnt a fuse or something before Hannah could be... anyway, burnt-out fuse, man. This guy would've kept on killing if it weren't for a burnt-out fuse."

"Burnt fuse... he would've killed for decades."

"Lucky, I guess."

"No such thing as luck. It was just his time."

Dixon swallowed and looked out over the parking lot. "You should know something." He paused. "Yesterday was my last day as a detective."

Baudin looked at him. "You're quitting?"

"I'm... transferring. The DA's office. I'm going to be a full-time investigator for them."

"The DA's office?"

He nodded.

Baudin's heart dropped. He felt ice in his guts. "That's why you got out. That's why those photos disappeared. You struck a deal with him."

"I'm not gonna spend the rest of my life in prison, man. I need to be with my wife and kid. They need me. What happened was a mistake, a terrible mistake, but it don't make nothin' better by having me rot away in a cell."

Baudin was on his feet now, though the pain of sudden movement made him wince. "What did he promise you?"

"This all goes away. But I have to work for him."

Baudin bent down to look into his eyes. "He's the devil, Kyle. Everything you became a cop to fight against."

Dixon shook his head. "I'm not gonna die in a prison cell."

"So you'd rather be his fucking hit man? That's why we had to go to the Walk farm, right? Sandoval saw Walk as a liability, and he sent us over to take him out, right? Tell me I'm fucking right, Kyle."

"You're right. It was a way for me to prove I'm loyal."

"Loyal?" Baudin turned away. He couldn't even look at him. "You can't do this, man."

"It's already done. The transfer's been approved. I just came to say goodbye."

Baudin turned and faced him. "And what if he has you do something that has me come after you? You gonna kill me, too, Kyle?"

He shook his head. "It's not like that."

"He fucking kills people that get in his way. That's the reason he became district attorney. It's the most powerful position in the county. This is his county, and you're kidding yourself if you think he won't kill anyone that stands up to him."

"It's this or prison, man. I won't do it. That kid needs me."

"Fuck you, Kyle." He got within an inch of his face. "Fuck. You. You and me, we're done."

48

Keri came one afternoon and picked Baudin up. He rushed out of the hospital without saying anything to anyone. He had no stomach for it. When he got into her car, he turned to her and kissed her passionately. The kiss felt so good, as if they were the only two people in the world and no one else mattered.

"Marry me," he whispered, pulling away.

"What?" she giggled.

"Marry me. I'm serious. Marry me right now, and let's move to California. Today."

"Ethan, we've only been—"

"Bullshit. You know. Everyone knows when it happens, and it happened to us. I know you feel it. We're supposed to be together. Marry me and move to California. I'm sick of this desert. I can't be here anymore. You tell me all the time how much you hate it. We'll get a condo on the beach, right on the water. You'll wake up every day to the sounds of the gulls and the waves rolling onto the sand. But we have to do it now. Marry me right now, and let's go. If we're here any longer, this place will suck us up. We'll take the girls out of school and go today. We can send for our stuff. Let's just go."

She held his gaze. Her eyes were beautiful, sparkling and blue. He wondered why he had never noticed them before that moment.

"Yes," she said.

He kissed her and didn't stop until someone honked behind them. She giggled and pulled the car forward. Baudin took the gold shield out of his pocket. He looked at it once then tossed it out the window as they pulled out of the hospital parking lot.

AUTHOR'S REQUEST

If you enjoyed this book, please leave a review on Amazon. I love hearing from my readers and reviews are great feedback as to what you want to see in future books.

So please leave a review and know that I appreciate each and every one of you!

Copyright 2015 Victor Methos

Print Edition

License Statement

This book is licensed for your personal enjoyment only. This book may not be re-sold or given away to other people. If you would like to share this book with another person, please purchase an additional copy for each recipient. If you're reading this book and did not purchase it, or it was not purchased for your use only, then please return to Amazon.com and purchase your own copy.

Please note that this is a work of fiction. Any similarity to persons, living or dead, is purely coincidental. All events in this work are purely from the imagination of the author and are not intended to signify, represent, or reenact any event in actual fact.

Printed in Great Britain
by Amazon